ONE LAST SHOT

ALEXANDRA WARREN

D1528637

One Last Shot (Nymphs & Trojans Book 2)
Copyright 2019 Alexandra Warren
Cover Art by Visual Luxe

All rights reserved. This book or any portion thereof may not
be reproduced or used in any manner whatsoever without the
express written permission of the publisher except for the
use of brief quotations in a book review.

This is a work of fiction. Any similarity to real locations,
people, or events is coincidental and unintentional.

ACKNOWLEDGMENTS

This is 30.

Wow.

To the **readers**, thank y'all SO much for the love, the notes of encouragement, the posts, the shares, the *everything.* Just… thank you. I'm forever grateful for all the support you guys have shown over these last few years on my journey to project #30.

To **my love**, who's been so supportive of my process with every book. Thank you. I love you.

To **CCJ**, who's literally been in my corner since day one of this author stuff. The one who pushed me off the ledge to publish. Sis, I don't know how we got here, but thank you lol

To my **sister-authors**, y'all have no idea how much y'all mean to me. The community, the support, the *talent.* Y'all are truly the best (with a special shoutout to LB for creating *Spilling That Hot Tea* and DW for letting me borrow *"The Zone"* lol)

And last but certainly not least, to **Nicole Falls**.
Girl.
Group projects have never *ever* been my thing, but collaborating with you has changed my mind lol. This process has been **so** much fun; creating this world, *and these people*, and channeling that collective creative energy into topics I know are so important to the both of us. Thank you for trusting me, thank you for keeping me going by leading the way, thank you for just… being you, honestly. I am so grateful that we embarked on this journey together, sis.

#NymphsAndTrojans 4eva.

SERIES NOTE

Books in the "Nymphs & Trojans" series can be read in any order. But if you haven't yet, I highly encourage you to check out Book 1 of the series, *Shots Not Taken* by Nicole Falls!

ONE

THEY SHOULD'VE USED his mugshot.

That was all I kept thinking as I stared at the professional headshot shared in the press release announcing that DeAndre "Dre" Leonard had been added to the Nashville Nymphs coaching staff as an assistant; a polished and pristine photo with just the right lighting and a charming crooked smile that told fans he could suddenly be trusted in this city again even though I knew better.

Really, we *all* should've known better.

I mean, it would be just like him to show up claiming he's ready to do right only to disappoint everyone… *again*. But leave it to the same front office who enabled his ass in the first place to bring him over to our side of the court like that would somehow make a difference, my eyes doing a slow roll on their own as I skimmed the article filled with bullshit quotes about how he saw a lot of potential in my team and hoped to bring the city another championship to match the one his squad, *the Tennessee Trojans,* won almost seven years ago - back when I was in love with him.

Admittedly, it was a one-sided affair since he didn't even know I existed unless he had a thing for top prospects in high school girls' basketball which I doubted. But as a senior getting ready to follow in his footsteps by attending Lynstone University where he'd only spent a year, I knew everything there was to know about him from his tendencies on the court to his tendencies outside of it, spending more time than reasonable watching his social media profiles like he was my boyfriend when really he was a total stranger, and I was just a fan.

Looking back, I might've been a little *too* obsessed. But it was hard not to be after watching someone come from nothing, use basketball to make something of himself, and help bring the Trojans a championship within their first couple of years of being an organization. He played my same position, had the endorsements I aspired to also have one day, and he was beloved in Nashville, making him something like my idol… *until he wasn't.*

The way he allowed himself to fall from glory so rapidly never made sense to me, a frown on my face as I thought about all the drama, and the drugs, and the mugshots that ultimately led to him being banned from the league for a couple of years. And to know that he was back, *here*, to coach us?

Yeah, I wasn't feelin' that at all, making plans to let that be known just as the head trainer, Ari, told me my time in the cold tub was up.

"You sure? You know I can go all day," I teased,

making Ari shake her head as she handed me a towel so I could dry off.

"Sit in there any longer and your pussy will turn into a popsicle," she joked, making me laugh as I quickly toweled off then tossed it back her way for her to catch with a joke of my own.

"*Good.* Maybe then someone will volunteer to eat it."

I was really just playing when I said it, but it was a fact that my "P.P." hadn't been tended to in far too long. *Well*, it hadn't been tended to by someone other than me in far too long, a puzzled look on my face as I struggled to remember the last time I even gave myself a tune-up as Ari replied, "You know exactly who wants to eat your pussy popsicle, but you playin'."

The fact that she even had the nerve to bring him up made me laugh again. "Ari, come on now. Kage is a baby. I might catch a case for just lookin' his way."

Okay, that might've been an exaggeration since Kage Steele was very much legal, very super fine, and rolling in dough thanks to his impressive first-round draft pick contract plus the endorsement deals that came with it. But he was still a baby, who was steady trying to be my baby according to Ari who was all smiles when she said, "Well that sure doesn't stop him from looking at you, Selena Samuels. You see what he said about you on *Twitter* today?"

My face scrunched on its own. "I thought they were going all *zero-dark-thirty* on social media like LeBron for the playoffs?"

"Yeah, until they lost last night. Zero-dark-thirty over," she replied, scrolling through her own phone and then handing it to me.

"Of course he'd be doing a damn Q&A with fans fresh off a

3

season-ending playoffs loss," I thought with an annoyed smirk, scrolling his tweets to see what Ari was talking about *and...*

"No this fool didn't," I groaned once I read the tweet that was a response to a fan asking who his favorite player of all-time was.

"Selena Samuels, no cap. Catch me front row at every Nymphs game this season ;)"

"That's not even the one I was talking about. Keep going," Ari urged, watching over my shoulder as I continued to scroll until I saw I was mentioned once again; this time by my nickname in response to someone asking who his celebrity crush was.

"The Sharpshooter. That's bae all day once she stops playin' with the kid."

"He must have a celebrity boo in the army or some-thin'," I reasoned, closing out of the app and handing Ari her phone back as she started to laugh.

"See what I mean? Quit making that boy chase the ice cream truck and pull over already."

Rolling my eyes, I exchanged my damp shorts for a pair of sweatpants as I told her, "I have bigger problems right now than being that little boy's Bugs Bunny ice cream."

"*With the gumball eyeballs*? Nah, sis. You're more like a... vanilla ice cream sandwich."

If a man would've ranked me as the most basic option on the side of the ice cream truck, I might've really been offended. But since Ari was something like a sister to me as far as the Nymphs organization went, I was all smiles when I playfully gushed, "*Wowwww*. A vanilla ice cream sandwich?! Really, Ari? I thought we were better than that. I mean, I'm at *least* a bomb pop. A bomb pop to represent this bomb pus…"

"*Anyway*," she cut me off, speaking over my giggles once she asked, "What are these bigger problems you speak of?"

Now I was the one scrolling through my phone, pulling up the press release I'd read in the cold tub and then handing it her way as I answered, "This."

Before she could even read the headline, she snapped her head back and groaned, "Good Lord, that man is *still* fine."

While I wholeheartedly agreed with her - I mean, *wholeheartedly* - I keep that to myself, quick to express, "That's not the problem, Ari. The problem is him being added to our coaching staff like he has any clue what our league is even about."

"Basketball is basketball, Selena," Ari rattled as she skimmed the article the same way I had before going back up to his picture to whisper, *"Unfairly fine"* prompting me to snatch my phone so that I could have her full attention when I offered my defense.

"But it's not. Over there, they're all flash, and dunks, and bravado. *But over here?* We really ball like a team, we play with skill and fundamentals, we… understand the privilege of this being an actual career and would never take that for granted the way he did."

"So is this about basketball, or is it about him personally?" she asked, her eyebrow piqued as she crossed her arms over her chest to challenge me.

With a shrug and not much thought, I replied, "I guess both. *I just...* I know there's a woman out there who really deserves this job. So to give it to him *is...*"

She cut me off with a laugh. "Girl, what's your angle here? Cause now you're on your women's rights shit, which I respect. But also, what is this *really* about? I mean, you don't think the man deserves a second chance?"

"Of course he deserves a second chance," I told her with a sigh, gnawing into my lip as I explained, "But experiencing the disappointment of his downfall from afar was enough. I don't need him coming up in here and dragging down the dynasty I'm trying to build too."

"Ahh, so that's what it is. You think his hiring is gonna fuck with your master plan to bring the city, *your city*, a championship?"

"Exactly," I answered, happy to see she was finally on the same page as me until she offered me a half-hearted smile meaning that might not have been the case after all.

"Sorry to break it to you, babe. But you can't score all the points, and coach the team, and work in the front office, and wash the jerseys. You have to work with people if you really wanna make that championship happen. And I doubt the Lloyds would've hired him if they didn't think he'd be able to help you do that."

"Or maybe Kat Lloyd just has a thing for light-skinned former ball players turned drug addicts," I countered, hoping that had something to do with it since some sort of physical attraction was the only thing that made sense to me.

I mean, in his heyday, he was definitely the type of guy you'd offer a job or something equivalent right after getting piped down, Ari enthusiastically agreeing with that thought according to the lust-filled look on her face when she replied, "No matter how you classify him, sis has good taste. Cause, *whew chi-lay*."

Instead of joining her in her daydream - *better yet, her Dre-dream* - I blurted, "I'm gonna go talk to her."

"And say what, Selena? According to that press release, it's a done deal."

"That may be true, but she's still gonna hear what I have to say about it," I replied, determinedly taking off towards the Nymphs offices as Ari stayed back with a groaned, "*In true Selena fashion…*"

It wasn't enough to stop me though, bypassing the offices of less important people to get to the one who actually mattered; the one that belonged to our majority owner and eldest daughter of the Lloyd family, Katianna better known as Kat.

Rumor had it that reviving the franchise and bringing it to Nashville to join the Trojans, which her family also owned, was all Kat's idea. And for that, she was good peoples in my book, taking a little bit of my edge off when I gently knocked on the door to get her attention.

"Kat, you got a minute?"

Peeking up from her laptop with a pleasant smile, she replied, "For my star player who already guaranteed me a championship, I have a few. What's on your mind?"

With her being so friendly, it was hard for me to keep the same energy I had with Ari, gnawing at the corner of my lip as I stepped a little further into her office to answer, "This new hire. Dre Leonard? Of all people?"

"What's wrong with Dre Leonard?" she asked with an immediate frown, making me wonder if my initial belief about there being something going on between the two of them was true as I chose my words carefully.

"Umm, let's start with the fact that the Trojans dropped him in his prime for a reason. *Lots of reasons*."

From the drugs, to the arrests and overall disregard for his obligation to his team, I could go on all day about just how unfit he was for the job. But instead of agreeing with my general concern, Kat brushed it off. "That was years ago, Selena. He's matured a lot since then. Paid the ultimate price of losing it all, got himself together, and now he just needs an opportunity. An opportunity that we, as a family, have decided to give him. The press is already eating it up."

"Of course they are," I thought with an annoyed groan, rolling my eyes as I told her, "Just great. The season starts in less than two weeks, and instead of talking about if we can make some magic happen with this year's squad, all the press coverage is going to him; *a man*. And we wonder why the league is in the shape it is now…"

From the way Kat sighed in response, I could tell she didn't totally disagree with my point. But that still didn't stop her from inquiring, "Why do you have such a problem with this? I thought you'd be in support of this particular hire."

No lie, if it wasn't affecting me, I'd probably be all

about the comeback kid story; tuned into the documentary on *Netflix*, or the special on *ESPN*, or whatever the media did to capture a moment like this. But because it *would* affect me… "In support of this particular hire for what? Because of his name? The same name that makes it very likely he'll be getting paid more than some of our rookies for doing a bunch of nothing while they're putting everything on the line night in and night out? The same name that allowed him to jump some very qualified women in the hiring line? He just gets to pop up in our league with no skin in the game other than his own failed career while the people who actually deserve a job like this gets skipped over. So no, I don't support this shit. I'm not with this shit. And I never will be."

My stance might've been harsh, but it was the truth. And I wasn't shying away from that until I heard a not-all-that-familiar voice behind me groan, "*Damn*. Tell me how you really feel."

Before I could say anything, *or even react at all*, Kat stood up from behind her desk to say, "Excuse her, Dre. She's not typically so…"

He cut her off. "Nah, I think she meant what she said exactly the way she said it, Kat. And you know what? She has a right to feel the way she feels."

Wait, what?

Turning around to see if I was imagining the whole thing, I came face to chest with who was once the man of my dreams. Though right now, it felt more like a nightmare as he looked down at me with those honey brown eyes of his to continue, "But let me tell you somethin', Ms. Samuels. No matter what you think you know about me, no matter how you feel about me, and no matter how long it takes for you to figure out we're here for the exact same thing, I'm not goin' anywhere."

Admittedly, I was a bit starstruck since this was the closest I'd ever been to my former idol, and I just wasn't prepared for so much fine. I mean, the perfectly-scruffy facial hair, the tattoos he couldn't hide if he wanted to, the height, the *smell*...

Even with the tiny inhale I took of his cologne, I managed to play it off, offering no more than a frown when I huffed, "*Hmph.* We'll see about that."

I expected him to return some of my attitude, but he didn't; only smiling a crooked smile and sending my body into a fury that forced me to end my impromptu meeting without a real solution since lusting after the new coach was definitely not going to help my cause. But even when I started to storm out, he called after me, "Oh, and Selena?"

Once I peeked back over my shoulder, I wished I hadn't, high school me wanting to squeal with excitement from the look on his face alone. But again, I was forced to hold it in, keeping my face neutral when he finally said, "It was nice to meet you too."

Since I couldn't exactly say the same - *and couldn't go full fangirl like his presence tempted me to* - I said nothing at all, continuing out of Kat's office back towards the training room to tell Ari what had happened. But unfortunately, the only person I ran into on my pursuit was the last one I felt like dealing with right now, a huge grin on his face as he said, "Well if it ain't Selena Mothafuckin' Samuels."

"Hey, Kage," I replied nonchalantly without breaking stride, hoping he'd catch the hint that I wasn't in the mood to entertain him.

Of course he didn't, changing his route in favor of mine when he asked, "You see the game last night?"

"I didn't," I lied, hoping that'd be enough to dead the conversation. But really, it only seemed to put a battery in his back as he started rattling off his stats that went in one ear and out of the other since one, I already knew them and two, I didn't really care right now.

Being completely honest, the only reason I hadn't told him to get out of my face was because he was so stinkin' cute; like a puppy that you would never buy for yourself but would gleefully pet the hell out of if it belonged to someone else. And with that on my mind, it was hard not to smile when I stopped to put a hand to his arm and told him, "Better luck next year, K."

He looked down at it like he couldn't believe I was actually touching him, an immediate smirk growing to his lips as he licked them to say, "I think you got a little more than just luck to offer me, Selena."

"Boy!" I squealed with a smack to his chest and a fit of giggles, not even pretending I wasn't tickled by the exchange as I left him in the dust while he shouted after me, *"Ready to make it real when you are, baby!"*

Shaking my head, I curled back into the training room to find Ari organizing her supplies, my continued giggles prompting her to peek up at me and comment, "From the smile on your face, I assume your little meeting with Kat went well."

With a toss of my hand towards where I'd just come from, I explained, "Nah, I just ran into Kage in the hallway."

Her eyebrow piqued. "And he's got you cheesin' like that? *Uh oh.* Sounds like somebody might be ready to pull the ice cream truck over after all."

That only made me giggle again. "Girl, no. He was just being silly."

"And you clearly enjoyed the jokes. *Mmhm*. You ain't low, Selena."

Since I knew it was just her nature to make something out of nothing, especially when it came to Kage, I brushed her off with an exaggerated, "*Anyway*. You won't believe what happened."

The look she responded with urged me to give her a quick rundown of my first interaction with Dre, doing a bunch of giggling of her own by the time I finished when she playfully scolded, "That's what your ass gets. But like, is he really as fine as he looked in that headshot?"

Now that he wasn't right in my face, I could let out how I truly felt, practically moaning when I thought about his full lips and admitted, "Finer than fine, Ari. Like, if Kat's riding that every night and hired him because of it, I can't even be mad."

That only made her giggle again. "So now you support the hire?"

"I didn't say all that. I just… understand it. Under those specific conditions," I clarified, honestly feeling a little bit jealous as I thought about Kat being able to wake up with the scent of his cologne on her sheets every morning.

Apparently, my jealousy was a bit premature since Ari was quick to remind me, "You mean, the specific conditions you made up in your head with no actual evidence to back it up?"

While she was right that there was nothing concrete I could point to to legitimize my claims, I still shared the one nugget I *had* picked up on during my ambush.

"The second I mentioned him, she jumped to his defense."

"Which sounds normal of a boss who truly believes in her hiring abilities. No one wants to be wrong about something like this, Selena," Ari replied, not only debunking my theory but also bringing whose side she was really on into question.

Crossing my arms over my chest, I asked, "So now you're on the Dre Leonard bandwagon too?"

Instead of fiercely speaking against it, she only shrugged. "I'm not on it. But I'm not off it either. I'm like, hanging out on the platform, but I haven't actually bought my ticket yet. Just peepin' the view. Weighing the pros and cons. Keeping an open mind."

Even if she didn't think so, her answer sounded more yes than no, making me purse my lips together in a frown as I grabbed my bag and groaned, "*Anyway*. I need to get home cause it's right back here tomorrow for media day, and Lord knows I'll need all the energy I can get to deal with both him *and* the press."

"You talkin' about Dre or Kage?" Ari asked, only making my frown grow tighter before I responded with the obvious.

"Dre. Why would I be stressed over Kage?"

From the immediate look of amusement on her face, I already knew what her angle would be, especially once she avoided my eyes to answer, "I mean, one day you're calling him silly and the next day he's going silly with his tongue on your pussy popsicle. Plus, I know a big dick strut when I see it, Selena. *And that one?* He should have a permit for all that he's carrying."

"Goodbye, Ari!" I squealed with a giggle on my way out, pulling my phone from my pocket to entertain myself for the walk from the arena to the parking garage until I heard a now *definitely* familiar voice calling after me.

"Selena, wait up."

Secretly, I wanted to pick up the pace and pretend like I hadn't heard him. But considering we were the only two in the area, I knew it would've been a stretch, forcing me to turn back his way where I found him standing a lot closer than I thought he'd be. I mean, a *lot* closer than I thought he'd be, literally towering over me when he started, "Look. We clearly got off on the wrong foot, and that ain't what I'm here for at all."

Taking a step back to create some space between us, I gripped into the crossbody strap of my duffle bag to ask, "What *are* you here for, Dre? Or should I call you Coach Leonard?"

"*Right now*? Dre is cool. But for media day, Coach Leonard will probably be best since they're known to be finicky about shit like that," he replied, offering advice I really didn't need as a veteran player before he continued, "Now to answer your original question, I'm here to help y'all win that championship I know you're after."

It sounded good, but I knew better than to fall for his words alone, cocking my head to the side to challenge, "And what exactly qualifies you to do that outside of your ring with the Trojans? You know, most people in your position settle for coaching their kids' little league team, or maybe even coaching at their old high school. Not this."

He shrugged, shoving his hands into his pockets as he replied, "I don't have any kids, so that knocks that first option off the list. And as far as my old high school goes… being back in my city ain't really good for me right now."

So many follow-up questions came to mind, but the only one I felt the need to get an answer to right now was, "And somehow being here *is* good for you?"

There was a flash of something dark in his eyes as he paused then nodded. "It's better. *I'm* better."

"Katianna Lloyd seems to think so too," I commented, adjusting my bag on my shoulder as I braced myself for Dre to put some more fuel into my little theory. And honestly, I *needed* him to put some fuel into my theory so my stares could be more business and less… *something else*.

The infectious chuckle he let off didn't help my cause at all, making it hard for me not to crack a tiny smile when he ran a hand over the top of his low fade and answered, "Yeah, I definitely owe her the naming rights of my firstborn or some shit for making this happen."

Again, tons of follow-up questions came to mind, with the top inquiry being, *"Y'all firstborn together, or…?"* But instead of allowing this conversation to go on any longer than it needed to, I deaded it completely, tossing a hand over my shoulder towards my truck as I told him, "*I*… need to get going. Beauty sleep and all that."

"You don't need much."

"*Excuse me?*"

Instead of owning up to his comment, he only smirked when he answered, "Nothin'. I'll see you tomorrow, Ms. Samuels," before taking off back towards wherever he'd come from. And even though I had just told him I needed to get going, I found myself stuck in place until he disappeared, trying to make sense of what had just happened.

I mean, did he really just…?

"Nah, you're trippin'," I decided, mainly so I could finally make a move to my truck. But the whole drive home, those simple four words that should've meant nothing remained on my mind, taunting current-me and pleasing fangirl-me all at once.

TWO

IT WAS ONLY DAY ONE, and I was already fuckin' up.

Having the star player of my new squad go in on me to upper management before I could even properly introduce myself to her was one thing. But lowkey checking for her after the fact?

Yeah, that shit wasn't in the plans at all.

I mean, before I'd officially joined the coaching staff, I was already pretty familiar with Selena Samuels. It was hard not to be considering what she was doing for the Nashville Nymphs organization and for the WNBA in general. But thinking she was kinda cute from afar was a lot different than seeing just how damn fine she was up close, her sienna brown skin, big doe eyes, and the braids she wore down to her ass making me feel things a coach definitely shouldn't be feeling for his player even though it wasn't like we were *that* far apart in age.

We'd lived very different lives over those years of difference though, with her spending four years in college and then taking her talents to the professional level for another three going on four now, and *me...* doing a lot.

Getting banned from the league for violating the drug policy. Going overseas to play and fuckin' that up too. Coming back to the states to discover I had damn near nothing to my name thanks to who I thought were my friends blowing money that wasn't theirs to begin with. Trying to rebuild from scratch and turning back to the stuff that got me in trouble in the first place when shit didn't work out right away. *Hitting a* new *rock bottom...*

Honestly, it was painful to even think about in general terms, so I tried not to as much as possible, instead focusing on the positive that was the Lloyd family taking a chance on me to become an assistant coach for their relatively new women's team after I successfully completed my twelve-step program and enrolled back in school.

When my former boss, Mr. Lloyd, said he had something for me whenever I was ready for it, an opportunity as grand as this was the furthest thing from my mind. But it was his belief - *his family's belief* - in me and my abilities that had me believing in myself again, fully-prepared to make the most of this coaching gig even if Selena didn't think I was worth a damn.

On a personal level, she could think whatever she wanted to. But on a professional level, I wasn't having that shit since I'd already learned the hard way what it was like when you wasted your chances. And being real, I couldn't afford it.

So if I had to repeatedly make that clear with her, it was what it was. As long as me repeatedly making that clear with her didn't turn into more of the lust-filled looks she liked to give even when she didn't realize she was giving them. It was almost like her head was telling her to hate me for whatever reason, but her heart was saying something different; a something different I couldn't put energy in decoding since doing something with that information almost guaranteed getting myself into some trouble.

Again, I couldn't afford that. But what I *could* afford was doing my job and staying in my lane which meant getting a good night's rest so that I was ready to take on the media the next day.

In my head, I was hoping they'd take it easy on me since it was going to be my first time really dealing with the unfiltered press as a coach. But in my gut, I had a feeling that wouldn't be the case since I'd never given a straight answer to the question everyone had been asking me for the last five or so years - *what happened?*

Kat had already coached me up on what to say, had given me strategies on how to redirect the conversation back to the Nymphs. But even with that, I was still nervous as hell as I made my way out onto the court that seemed a little empty compared to what I was expecting - or rather, what I had grown used to over with the Trojans.

There were still enough people to have me shook though, my shoulders tense as I felt a gentle hand against my lower back followed by an even gentler voice asking, "Ready to do this, Coach?"

Peeking down, I found the head coach of the Nymphs, Sugar Daniels, looking up at me with the most pleasant smile like she knew I needed it, bringing me some relief as I admitted, "Not quite, but I'll rise to the occasion."

If there was anyone who understood that phrase, it

was Sugar who had spent her whole life rising up to folks trying to play her for just barely being over five foot tall. But what she lacked in height, she made up in passion and effort that carried her through college ball, a stint playing professional, and then some time in front of the camera as an analyst and commentator for both leagues before the Nymphs snatched her up to coach last year.

Nodding with understanding, she replied, "I know this ain't your first time to the rodeo, Dre. But just remember, these folks have a special sixth sense for bull-shit and will happily press you on it with follow-up questions; especially if it's something exclusive that'll make their little blog pop."

"Trust me, I couldn't forget that if I wanted to cause I've *definitely* made some shit pop off in the past."

Of course, those weren't my proudest moments, but it was the truth. A truth that made her chuckle when she assured, "You'll do great."

"Appreciate it, Sugar," I quietly replied as we both directed our attention to the makeshift press conference set up once Kat tapped the mic to get everyone's attention then gave an introduction.

"Welcome to the *official* Nashville Nymphs media day. We're happy to have you all joining us and look forward to your continued coverage throughout the season. Now, first to take questions will be our head and assistant coach, Sugar Daniels and DeAndre Leonard, followed by our starting veteran trio, and finally our two rookies. After that, all coaches and players, including the reserves, will be available for one-on-ones."

Like it was news to me, I started nodding along with the rest of the media members present until I saw Kat waving Sugar and I to the front, the gesture making me swallow hard as I followed Sugar's lead and took the seat labeled with my name for the first time in what felt like forever.

Somehow, it still felt like home.

Being in front of the press, sitting behind a mic to take questions, it still felt... *familiar.*

And you would've thought everyone could read my mind since the first question posed to me after the reporter rattled off his name and credentials was, "Dre, how does it feel to be back in Nashville under a new title?"

An easy smile came to my lips as I answered, "It feels great. I'm extremely grateful for Kat and the rest of the Lloyd family giving me this opportunity, and I'm excited for the season to get underway."

"Why the Nymphs and not the Trojans?"

If I hadn't prepped for this shit with Kat, the question might've tripped me up. But because we had, *extensively*, my easy smile remained as I told him, "I take opportunities as they come, and this was the one presented to me."

"But wouldn't you rather be with the Trojans? Or did they not want you after your ban was lifted?" he pressed, making me cringe even though it was expected since... *of course they'd want to talk about the ban.*

Releasing a heavy sigh, I parted my lips to give my rehearsed answer until I saw Sugar lean towards her mic to respond, "When Dre's name came up, I jumped at the chance to add him to my staff before the Trojans could even think about it. The ban he faced as a player was an unfortunate situation. But that ban didn't eliminate his ability to see the court in ways none of us can, a skill that will aid us tremendously as we battle to get this team back to the playoffs and beyond."

Her gesture was unexpected but greatly appreciated, especially since it directed the attention off of me and onto her as another reporter listed her credentials then asked, "Sugar, now that you've officially gotten a season under your belt as head coach, how are you feeling about the Nymphs chances to do exactly what you just said in getting back to the playoffs?"

"We've already done it. Now we're moving onto bigger goals," Sugar answered confidently, prompting the reporter to follow with, "As in a championship?"

"As in *multiple* championships. Enough to fill this arena with so many gotdamn banners that the Trojans are forced to hang theirs somewhere else."

The media members chuckled at that, and I did too, admiring how easily she was able to work them until I caught a glimpse of Selena heading to the court and immediately started admiring her fine ass as she stood in the back waiting for her turn to take the mic. Somehow her being in full uniform only added to her appeal, with the top half of her braids pulled back into a ponytail and her face fully made up for the team and individual photos we'd be taking later.

She looked like a superstar.

She *was* a superstar.

And when they asked me how I felt about her as a player, I didn't hold back on expressing that, taking a page out of Sugar's book when I joked, "Not only is Selena a dynamic talent, but she's also a Lynstone alum which automatically puts her ahead of the class," earning myself a murmur of chuckles before I continued, "But seriously, I'm excited to be able to work with a player of her caliber. A player with a presence big enough to change the game and the mindset of a champion."

Even from a distance, I could see the flattered look on Selena's face as she gnawed at the corner of her lip while the reporters went on to ask Sugar and I a few more questions before we were finally dismissed. And with our dismissal came the introduction of Selena along with two other core veteran players, Selena catching me in passing with a hand to my arm to whisper, "You looked good up there, Coach Leonard. Like you might actually belong."

"And yet I still got a feelin' you bouta show me how it's done," I whispered back with a smirk that only had Selena glowing even brighter as she moved to take the middle seat between her teammates to take questions while I posted up in the back to listen.

Like Sugar, Selena was a natural at dealing with the spotlight, with enough charisma and charm to carry all three of them since the other two looked like they'd rather be anywhere else than here. Selena seemed to revel in it though, all smiles until a reporter asked how she felt about me being added to the coaching staff.

Because of what I'd walked in on yesterday in Kat's office, I wasn't surprised to see her light dim a little bit when she took a quick glance at me before she answered, "Even though Coach Leonard's career here as a Trojan didn't end on good terms, he still knows this court. He knows this city and what winning a title would mean to it since, *well*, he's already been there and done that. And he knows the game, which to me is the only thing that really matters."

I couldn't help the way my eyebrow piqued in shock

as Selena took another glance my way and gave a pleasant smile while the reporter followed up, "Well we found a clip on *Youtube* of an interview you did senior year before the *McDonald's* All-American game. And in that, you called Dre your favorite player. Is that still true?"

Teasingly cocking my head to the side to ask the same question, I couldn't help but chuckle once I saw Selena's nose and lips twist when she replied, "I mean… he's *aight*," making everyone else chuckle too as she admitted, "In all honesty, I can say my game changed for the better because of his example. And I feel lucky to now have access to more… hands-on lessons."

The shit was wrong as fuck, but I couldn't help the rise I got out of her word choice, adjusting in my stance as Selena gave me another quick glance just as Kat put an arm to my elbow to say, "Dre, we need you over here for pictures."

Before I could really respond, she was already tugging me in that direction. And it was a good thing she was since I wasn't sure how quick I would've been ready to move otherwise, completely enthralled watching Selena work her magic on the press - watching Selena, *period* - which was the absolute last thing I should've been doing.

"You can't afford that, bruh," I reminded myself as I posed for my individual shots, then posed for a few shots with Sugar and the rest of the coaching staff. And as we waited for the rookies who were now taking questions from reporters, Selena came over to do her individual shots, forcing me to find something to keep myself busy since I couldn't get caught up in watching her again.

With my phone in my hand, I scrolled through

Twitter to see I'd already been tagged in random pictures and soundbites from today. And once I refreshed the feed, I saw someone had just shared the clip of Selena talking about me, clicking to view it like I hadn't just heard it live and smiling to myself as I watched her speak confidently about my abilities to get the job done.

Did she even believe the shit she was saying?

I wasn't sure.

But after yesterday, her being able to give me a compliment without choking on her words was enough to satisfy me as I peeked up from my phone and was immediately drawn in by her practically flirting with the camera as she dribbled the basketball and loudly joked, "Anything for ticket sales, y'all!"

Everyone in listening range started to laugh, including Sugar who moved a little closer to me to say, "Sometimes it's hard to believe that silly ass girl is actually a savage."

With a shake of my head, I disagreed. "Shit, it ain't hard for me at all after I caught a glimpse of her savage ass yesterday when she chewed me out to Kat."

That made Sugar laugh. "I heard about that. Don't take it personal, Dre. Selena's just very... *protective* of our organization; very protective of our game overall."

Knowing what I knew about how the general public viewed the WNBA, I could totally understand why she'd be that way, the thought alone making me nod as I replied, "Yeah, I get it."

"And between you and me, I think part of that animosity is because she has a little crush on you," Sugar added, the shit catching me off-guard as I coughed up a, "*What?*"

Again, she laughed. "Don't act all surprised, Dre.

You may not be all that dark, but you're still tall and handsome. And if you were a few years older, you'd be easy bait. Don't go runnin' to HR with that, though."

Now I was the one chuckling, turning her way to tease, "*Thee* Sugar Daniels said she'd get at me if I had a little more mileage on me, and I'm supposed to be offended by it?"

Instead of answering the question, she reached up to give me a pat on the shoulder and said, "I think we're gonna get along just fine, Coach Leonard."

"I think so too, Coach Daniels," I agreed, calling after her to add, "Oh, and Coach? Thanks for that save earlier. Your answer was a helluva lot better than mine."

Sure, mine would've been sufficient. But hers made me truly feel supported in my role, a feeling she only doubled down on when she replied, "You're one of us now, Dre. And if nothing else, we take care of our own."

I gave her a nod of acceptance that sent her on her way just as a journalist approached and asked, "Dre, if you don't mind. We'd like to get a few shots of you and Selena for a piece we're doing based around that *Youtube* clip."

Once again, I found myself nodding as I followed him onto set, Selena shooting me a playful side eye the second I joined her in front of the lights then leaning over to whisper, "You don't have to stand so close to me, ya know."

"I think that's kinda the point of them doing pictures of us together, Ms. Samuels," I told her with just as much tease as we waited for more instructions from the photographer who returned to set with a stool in his hand.

"Dre, we're gonna have you sit on this, and Selena

we'll have you kinda lean in and rest your forearms on top of his left shoulder," he directed, the two of us doing our interpretation of his request as he returned behind the camera to do a few test shots that eventually turned into real shots where he asked us to loosen up a little bit.

With Selena over my shoulder, I couldn't really see what she was doing. But I knew she wouldn't be able to keep a straight face when I joked, "All that dribbling from earlier got you kinda musty."

Immediately, she busted out laughing in my ear and squealed, "*Oh my*... shut up!" as the photographer cheered, "*Yes! Perfect! Keep that up!*" And I suppose now that I had broken the ice, Selena was ready to do the same, doing a little joking of her own when she said, "Don't be using these pictures with me to get your likes up on *Instagram*."

Shaking my head without totally disrupting the perfect lighting, I told her, "Nah, the ladies don't tend to "like" when I post women who aren't them on my page."

One of the photographer's assistants passed me a ball to add to the shots as a prop. But before I could adjust it myself, Selena leaned over my shoulder to do it for me, making sure the new *WNBA* logo was front and center while also replying, "I'm not talking about from women, Dre. I'm talking about the men who are guaranteed to come through with a "like" and hit you with a, "*I see you, bro*" in the comments that you'll have to correct them on."

"Or will I?" I asked, not even really realizing how wrong the question could be taken until I saw the surprised look on Selena's face as her candid smile turned anxious.

"*Wait. I didn't mean it like...*" I started; though it fell on deaf ears since Selena was already stepping away to ask the photographer, "You got enough pictures, right?"

"Plenty," he happily replied, giving Selena all the permission she needed to rush off set. And since it was clear I'd made her uncomfortable, I started to go after her until Kat caught me by the arm with a groaned, "*Nope.* Not letting you do that."

"What are you talkin' about, Kat?" I asked with a frown, knowing my intentions were only to clear the air and explain why I preferred not to give the trolls in my comments any attention at all.

But Kat already had her mind made up about the interaction, being sharp and direct when she answered, "Leave her alone, Dre. That's all I'm gonna say about it. Do your job and leave that girl alone."

Shaking my head, I sighed, "It's not even like that." And, *for the most part*, that was the truth.

Though from the displeased look on Kat's face, she clearly didn't believe me at all, stepping closer to keep the conversation between us when she challenged, "Dude, I stood behind the camera during those shots y'all just did together. And the way you looked at her? It's *definitely* like that. And it can't be like that unless you wanna cause a PR nightmare for all parties involved. Understood?"

She was right.

It was only my second real day on the job, and the last thing I needed was a bunch of rumors about me circulating already; especially rumors involving the damn star player of the team. So instead of continuing to defend myself, I only nodded. "Yeah, I hear you."

My response must not have been enthusiastic

enough for her since she got right in my face to emphasize, "Dre, I'm not kidding. I need you focused on
basketball and basketball only. And I'll be sure to have
this same conversation with Selena."

"That won't be necessary," I insisted, knowing I'd
already creeped Selena out enough on my own.

But again, Kat wasn't leaving it up to me, quick to
reply, "Oh, but it's happening anyway. And you wanna
know why? Cause I saw the way she looked at you too."

My eyebrow piqued on its own since… *how* did *she
look at me?*

I mean, sure we'd found our groove and joked
around a bit for the purposes of the photoshoot, but I
hadn't necessarily caught a vibe from her. Then again,
why would Kat make it up?

Instead of wondering, I decided to put it all in the
back of my mind and focus on the task at hand of
finding my spot in the back row for team pictures, being
sure to stand opposite of where Selena was sitting in the
front so my boss would know her message was received.
But not even that was enough to stop Kat from whispering to Selena about something that I had a feeling
involved me.

THREE

WHEN KAT ASKED me to stop by her office before I left the arena, I wasn't sure what to expect. But I damn sure wasn't expecting her to indirectly tell me to stay away from her man under the guise of keeping things "appropriate" with Coach Leonard as if I'd done anything to even hint otherwise.

She called herself being polite about it too, with her hands interlocked on top of her desk and a pleasant, professional smile on her face when she explained, "It's important for you guys to have a good working relationship. But we'd hate to give fans the impression that there's… something more going on between the two of you."

No matter how she packaged it, I was still annoyed when I defended, "I literally just met the man, Kat. Where is this even coming from?"

"I'm just making my… *the organization's* expectations clear, Selena. That's all," she replied, her professional smile intact as if she hadn't let that "my" slip.

"Yeah, this is definitely not about the organization or *the*

fans," I thought as I leaned forward in my chair to ask, "So, wait. Yesterday, you wanted me to be more supportive of the new hire. And now, because I'm not going at his neck, you're accusing me of being *too* supportive?"

With a slow glide of her tongue across the top row of her teeth, she cocked her head to the side and straight up asked, "Is flirting with your coach in front of the camera really what you consider support?"

No lie, the question had me a bit shook since I hadn't expected her to be so bold about it. And even though I could admit Dre and I had *maybe* gotten a little more comfortable with each other on set, my face still scrunched when I repeated, "*Flirting*? Are you being serious right now? Cause I feel like you're tryna play me."

"Look at these preliminary shots they got of you two for that feature, and ask me that question again," she insisted, sliding her *iPad* my way to show me what she was talking about. And honestly, with the pictures in my face, I could see why she felt the way she did.

I mean, Dre and I looked *disgustingly* cute together, every picture somehow looking better - *and more adorable* - than the last. Though I still tried to play it down when I scrolled nonchalantly and commented, "The photographer did a great job."

"*Selena…*" she groaned, my eyes flashing up to hers as I snapped, "What? I can't help that we're both fine."

"Oh, so you *do* think he's fine?" she asked with a scowl that told me this conversation had officially crossed over from professional to personal.

Still, that didn't mean I was going to lie about it, shrugging when I answered, "I mean, I'm not blind,

Kat. But just because I think he's fine doesn't mean I like, want him. Is that what you think? That I want him?"

Instead of answering my question, she pressed, "Well... do you?"

Without even letting a beat pass, I firmly replied, "I do not."

Maybe in my past life, I would've been all over him. *But right now?*

I didn't really have time for that, especially since it was clear Katianna already had her claws in his tattoos by the way she demanded, "So act like it. That's all I... *we're* asking."

Since any confrontation beyond this was unnecessary, I only nodded as I told her, "I got you, boss," standing up from my seat to ask, "Can I go now?"

"Yeah, I'll see you tomorrow," she replied dismissively, the whole thing making me roll my eyes the second I turned away from her to leave. And as I continued my way towards the parking garage, I pulled out my phone to shoot Ari a text.

"Whew, shit. Kat just went full Nivea on ya girl." - Selena

By the time I made it to my truck, I had a response.

"Nivea? Like the lotion?" - Ari

"No, fool. The singer. You know, "Don't Mess With My Man" Nivea." - Selena

Just the thought of the song had me pulling it up on my phone so I could blast it through the *Bluetooth* speakers on my drive home, laughing to myself as I sang along with the same conviction I used to sing it with back in the day even though I had no man then - *or* now.

Damn.

Being a good driver, I waited until I hit a red light to check Ari's latest message.

"So she actually claimed Dre?" - Ari

"Basically. Accused me of flirting, asked me straight up if I wanted him, told me if I act up, I'ma get smacked up." - Selena

"SHE SAID THAT?!" - Ari

Because of the light turning green, I didn't get a chance to respond right away. And apparently that delay built too much anticipation for Ari since, when I finally checked my phone at another red light, I found she'd sent the exact same message again, this time with extra question marks.

"SHE SAID THAT?!?!????" - Ari

"Not that last one. But the first two, yes." - Selena

"Still wild. I can't believe she really came at you like that." - Ari

Honestly, I couldn't believe it either, the whole thing feeling out of character for Kat who was usually so put together. But then I considered the circumstances, and it all started to make more sense, something I was sure to address when I finally made it home and responded to Ari.

"Girl, I don't know what his dick did to her. But if a dick makes me act like that… I WANT IT! LMAO just kidding, just kidding." - Selena

"LOL! You're definitely not kidding..." - Ari

Leaning against my kitchen island, I keyed an honest reply.

"I am though. Kat's usually so badass. So for her to come at me on some woman-to-woman shit claiming that it's only business is kinda wack." — Selena

"Maybe it really is just business, Selena. I mean, from her perspective, the star player fuckin' around with the new assistant coach would definitely be bad optics." - Ari

Because I knew for a fact we weren't - *and wouldn't be* - fuckin' around, it was hard for me to see it her way. But after taking a moment to get over myself, I understood it a little better; though that still didn't stop me from reminding Ari of my theory when I responded.

"And the chairman/owner of the team fuckin' around with the new assistant coach is somehow better?" - Selena

"Not better. But not as bad as situation A." - Ari

I hated to admit it, but Ari had a point; especially when I thought about some of the other inter-organization relationships currently happening around the league.

"**You're right. Cause the VP and the head coach up in Minnesota are definitely married with a son and no one cares. Hell, two teammates in Chicago just got married too. So basically all of this could be avoided if I was into women. Maybe I should consider it.**" - Selena

"**Girl... Goodnight!**" - Ari

I thought about sending her the scissors emoji to fuck with her, but decided I'd already gotten on her nerves enough for one night, leaving my phone on the counter as I went to take a long, hot shower then spent another fifteen minutes on my nighttime facial routine since being overseas up until three weeks ago had did a number on my skin. It was really an unfair schedule, playing in the states four months out of the year and then spending another seven playing in a foreign country. But it was what was expected and what kept my bank account happy, so I did what I had to do, luxuriating in the expensive skincare products I was able to afford because of it before calling it a night.

Well… I got in the bed and turned off the lights with plans of calling it a night. But unfortunately, my body still hadn't quite adjusted to my hometown time zone, sending me tossing and turning until I finally gave in to wasting time on my phone.

Turning down the brightness of my screen, I started on *Instagram*, scrolling the feed and giving a few "likes" before scrolling back up to the top to watch the stories.

One of the rookies, Mikayla Newsome, had chronicled most of media day which included a video of me being silly during my solo shots followed by a scan of the court that showed… *wait.*

Starting the video from the beginning, I held my finger down on the screen to pause it when I saw Coach Sugar and Dre huddled up watching me. Naturally, I wondered what they were talking about, wondered if she was giving Dre the same kind of warning Kat had given me. But instead of giving it much thought, I let the video play on, smiling to myself when I discovered the next clip was of Mikayla gassing up our fine ass new assistant coach.

"Got Coach Leonard up in here on his *GQ* shit. I see you, boy!" she cheered, making Dre laugh that adorable rumbling chuckle of his as he replied, *"You crazy, Mik,"* before it jumped to the next clip of Dre and I on set during the mini-shoot we'd done together.

The caption read, *"Current Nymphs Finest x Former Trojans Finest. I Stan."* And while I tried not to be bothered by it since it wasn't exactly a lie, I was completely caught off-guard when I discovered the next clip was a selfie-style video of Mikayla explaining the footage of the two of us to her followers.

"So some of y'all hit my DMs asking about Selena and Coach Leonard. As far as I know, they are not a couple even though I'm hella *ready to 'ship 'em after today. Guess y'all will just have to tune in this season to see what happens."*

The way she said it hinted at a possibility of it being at all true. And while that was enough for me to at least make plans of addressing her at practice about it the next day, the need to check her became immediate when

I saw she'd shared a poll with the question, *"Which ship name y'all rockin' with? SeAndre or Delena?"*

Instead of placing my vote for either so I could see the results, I replied to the post.

"OMG! Delete this!" - **@SharpshooterSS**

Glancing at the time at the top of my screen, I realized she probably wouldn't see the request until the morning, giving the video plenty of time to make its rounds before she'd even be able to take it down. But to my surprise, the message was read only a few short moments later, Mikayla replying, **"It's good promo! And weren't you the one yelling about anything for tickets sales earlier?"**

"Yes. But starting rumors about me is where I draw the line." - **@SharpshooterSS**

"Where YOU draw the line. But as for the rest of us who are still working to build their following and have an impact on this organization… ;)" - **@MikkiNews**

I don't know why she thought a wink emoji would make me feel any better, but it didn't. In fact, I was so annoyed that I sat up in bed to type out my reply.

"Don't be surprised when you catch an "accidental" elbow to the gut tomorrow, little girl." - @SharpshooterSS

My threat was supposed to be at least a *little* intimidating. But it was clear I had been way too nice to these new girls once I read her responses.

"That's a bet ;)" - @MikkiNews

"Oh. And because I know you're wondering, SeAndre is currently in the lead with 65% of the vote. Good night, Selena!" - @MikkiNews

"Definitely being too nice," I whispered in the darkness, already thinking of another way I could torture her ass at practice as I went to watch her story again since I might've been a little obsessed with the footage of Dre and I. I mean, the clip was only a few seconds long, but it was still long enough for me to understand why everyone was speculating about our involvement.

We looked... like a pair. Or like we could be a pair, under different circumstances. But it was our current circumstances that had me not only clicking out of the app, but also out of my phone completely, forcing myself to sleep knowing that could never be.

I'd gone too far.

I was only supposed to be making a point to Mikayla that my threats weren't baseless. But I hadn't expected that the little extra "umph" I put in boxing her out to get a rebound during practice would have her fragile ass curled up in the fetal position with Coach Sugar and Ari huddled over her trying to figure out exactly what was wrong.

"My stomach," she groaned breathlessly from the ground, making me feel a little bad for purposely knocking the wind out of her even though she deserved it for that shit she put on social media about me yesterday. And with that on my mind, that little bit of guilt I felt turned nonexistent as I left the court to go get some water.

Squirting a sip from the bottle into my mouth, I damn near choked when I saw Dre headed my way with a pleased smirk, looking way too fine in his casual coach gear of a cardinal red Nymphs dri-fit t-shirt and matching basketball shorts with a whistle hanging from his tattooed neck. I mean, he'd been around for the entire practice, so I shouldn't have even been fazed by his presence. But I'd also been in the competitive zone which meant I hadn't noticed him the way I did now that he was right in my face, grabbing a bottle for himself as he teased, "Didn't read you to be the hazing type, Ms. Samuels."

There was a hint of amusement in his tone like I'd done the shit for fun which wasn't the case at all, something I clued him in on when I replied, "If you knew what she said about us, you'd haze her ass too."

"About us?"

Turning his way to see his eyebrow piqued in confusion, I released a heavy sigh as I explained, "Yes, about us. As in me and you. DeAndre and Selena. Apparently we're a topic of discussion around these parts."

Instead of being surprised like I expected him to be, he released a sigh of his own. "Yeah, I already heard it from Kat. I don't know why people love making shit up."

"Of course he'd heard it from Kat," I thought, using the corner hem of my practice jersey to wipe the sweat off my nose as I ranted, "Me neither. I mean, two fine mothafuckas get in close proximity of each other, *and…*"

"*Wait.* Two fine mothafuckas?" he interrupted with another smirk, making me tense up since I'd *definitely* let that one slip.

It wasn't a lie, though. And because of that, I didn't back down when I shrugged to reply, "I mean, I know I'm fine. And you aren't exactly ugly."

For whatever reason, that made him laugh. "Nah, you called me a fine mothafucka. That's a title reserved for the *especially* handsome, Selena. Not for some ol' regular, casually attractive nigga."

I hated how right he was, hated how *non-regular* his attractiveness was now that he had rebounded from those awful mugshots I last remembered him by. In those, I could tell the drugs had started to take a toll on his body, with his already lanky frame appearing even thinner than normal and his eyes partially sunken in. But now, he looked… *healthy*, and happy, and good enough to have me blushing the longer he stared at me waiting for a response.

"Stop looking at me like that before you get us in trouble," I told him in a tone that was so obviously flirtatious it made me sick as I turned to see Mikayla finally getting up from the ground under her own power.

Thank God.

With a nod, Dre turned to watch the same scene I was as he agreed, "You right. Especially since I should be reprimanding your ass for that cheapshot you just gave Mikayla."

"She'll be aight," I told him with another shrug, putting my water bottle down so I could head back onto the court until I realized what he had insinuated; that he already had the authority to punish me.

"Do you really think you have that kinda power around here? Cause *uh...* nah, bruh. You gotta earn your stripes just like the rest of us," I told him with a laugh, finally making my move back towards the court until he called after me.

"In that case, I'll see you after practice."

Wait, what?

Turning back his way, I frowned. "You'll see me after practice for what?"

I expected to see at least a hint of the playfulness he'd had about him before. But there was none, not a single ounce when he glared at me and replied, "For the one-hundred three-pointers you owe yourself. Your shooting percentage from behind the arc was trash overseas, and we can't have that carrying over into our season."

A flurry of feelings rushed over me as I played his words back in my head. I mean, my instincts were to be offended since he'd put me and "trash" in the same phrase. And of course I wanted to be annoyed since staying after to shoot extra shots meant more stress on my body when I was supposed to be taking it easy as I

43

recovered from the overseas season. But the fact that he'd done his homework to even know I had struggled from behind the arc meant something. The fact that he was volunteering his time to put in extra work with me meant something. The fact that he'd referred to it as "our season" like his investment in our team was genuine meant something.

For those reasons, it was hard for me to really be upset about his request. But that didn't mean I wasn't going to put a little stank on it when I tightened my eyes and agreed, "*Fine*. I'll be there."

FOUR

THE *VICTORY LAP* album blared from the practice court's speakers as I watched Selena rest with her hands on her thighs working to catch her breath, somehow looking even finer than usual now that she was dripping in sweat from her first three rounds of twenty three-point shots. After the first round, she'd decided to ditch her practice jersey, leaving her in just a sports bra and her practice shorts which only made it harder for me to ignore just how fuckin' attractive she was. But because she was also working her ass off, I did my best to *at least* put it in the back of my mind when I finally asked, "You ready to go again?"

We were past the halfway mark, but I could tell the extra work was starting to take a toll on her by how tired she was. And because of that exhaustion, she only nodded in response to my question, wiping her sweaty hands on her shorts and then getting them in position to catch the basketball as I passed it her way to begin round four.

Unfortunately, it only took a few shots for me to

realize we were hustling backwards since, by this point, her legs and arms were so weak that she was barely hitting the rim. So after securing the rebound, I kept the ball to myself instead of passing it her way for another shot.

"Aight, aight. We can shut it down."

"But I'm not done," she whined, a frown on her face like she couldn't believe I was really cutting her off.

I wasn't fazed, though. In fact, I couldn't help but chuckle a little bit as I reminded her, "Selena, you just bricked five in a row, and that was *after* a break. Let's not burn you out."

Instead of taking my advice, she snapped, "I said I'm not done, Dre."

I knew what was in her best interest, but I also knew it was in my best interest not to argue with her, releasing a heavy sigh as I launched the ball back her way fully expecting her to repeat the same poor performance she'd just put on. But to my surprise, she was completely locked in, hitting seventy-percent of her remaining shots and ending on an all-net make that had an, *"I told you so,"* smirk etched on her face.

Since we weren't in competition with each other by any means, I smirked myself as I acknowledged, "Counting just those last fifteen, that was the best you've shot all day."

"Told you I wasn't done. Now come on. Let me knock these last twenty out," she urged, moving to the next spot and getting her hands ready for the final round. And this time, I wasn't as surprised when she breezed through them with a confident expression on her face, shooting a solid sixteen-for-twenty and ending on another make that had her hyped as she celebrated with the perfectly-timed lyrics, *"Dedication. Hard work plus patience."*

"What you know about that Nipsey Hussle?" I asked over my shoulder on my way to the sideline, plopping down on one of the bench seats as Selena made her way over to do the same.

Sitting with a seat in between us instead of taking the one next to me, she used a towel to pat her face dry as she answered, "I know enough for my heart to ache every time I think about him being gone."

With a nod, I agreed, "Yeah, I feel that. Good shit on that last round, though."

"I don't like being counted out, Dre. Don't let it happen again," she scolded, only making me chuckle once more.

"Nah, I *will* let it happen again cause it seems to be just the fire you need to push through when you get tired."

Instead of agreeing, she only shook her head with a playful grin on her lips that didn't exactly match the, "I really don't like you," coming out of them.

Shrugging, I slouched back in my seat and reminded her, "Established that from day one. Anything else you need to get off your chest?"

"There is this one thing…" she trailed, gnawing into her lip in a way that already had me intrigued as I sat back up to address it.

"What's on your mind?" I asked, not at all expecting the question that she turned my way to respond with; the question I'd heard endlessly.

"What happened to you, Dre? I mean, really. What happened?"

There was a legitimate look of concern on her face

that, for whatever reason, had me feeling less cagey than usual about the whole thing. And even though I really didn't owe her an explanation, I decided to give her the truth anyway, biting down on the inside of my cheek before I answered, "My grandmother passed."

"I'm assuming you two were really close?"

"*Extremely*. She basically raised me since my mom was in and out, and I never knew my dad," I shared, glancing out towards the court instead of looking at her when I continued, "I mean, don't get me wrong, I was bullshittin' before that happened. Just on some typical young nigga who just came into some money shit. But, that's what really sent me spiraling. Pulling my phone out after we'd just won the championship and finding a bunch of missed calls from the hospital trying to get in touch with me. By the time I called back, she was already gone."

Speaking the shit out loud had my throat tight as I bit down on my cheek once again, Selena moving to take the seat next to me and putting a gentle hand against my forearm to say, "I'm so sorry, Dre."

"Yeah, I was too. Feeling like I could've done more, or like I should've left her in better care, or... *something*. Anything than letting my moms look after her," I sighed, remembering how angry I felt when I learned my mom had been using the money I'd been giving her to cover my grandmother's needs on her own habits.

In hindsight, it might not have been the wisest decision to put her in control of the finances since my mom was known to be flaky as hell. But the truth, "*I just... I* thought I could trust her, you know. Thought she was different. But she wasn't, and my grandma suffered because of it. My grandma died because of it."

"Dre, I'm so…" Selena started before I turned back her way to cut her off.

"Nah, no need to keep apologizing. I've made peace with it for the most part. At least that aspect of it. The rest of it was on me, and rebuilding from that is something I'm still working on daily."

"You're talking about the drug problem?" she asked, her words making me tense up since a huge part of my daily work was truly forgiving myself for ever going down that path to begin with.

I mean, a little weed here and there was no biggie. But allowing much harder shit to take over, *destroy*, my life like I hadn't been a witness to what it had done to my mother?

It didn't make sense. Then again, with genetics and circumstances considered, it *did* make sense. Especially when I thought of how it all came about, something I tried to explain to Selena when I answered, "More so the pain and anxiety I tried to cover up by using. After that stuff with my grandmother and mom, I became paranoid, like I couldn't really trust anybody. And to mask that, I used "prescription pain killers" to the point of getting myself kicked out of the league in my fuckin' prime. Then when I came back from my failed attempt at hooping overseas, I realized that paranoia wasn't for nothin' since the niggas I thought were my friends turned out to be just as grimy which only made me even more paranoid. It was like everybody I knew became the enemy overnight, and the only way to block that out was to keep experimenting with shit I had no business even touching to begin with."

Thinking back on that time in my life, it was honestly a blessing that I'd even recovered since things were *beyond* bad. My health wasn't in good shape, my pockets were thin, I had nothing to look forward to, nothing to live for. But when Selena asked, "What saved you?" my energy changed instantly, the turning point being something I'd never forget and bringing a half-hearted smile to my lips.

"*Honestly?* The Lloyds," I shared, watching her eyebrow pique in surprise as I explained, "I'd always had a pretty good relationship with Mr. Lloyd. And one day, he hit me up on some random shit just to see how I was holding up and could immediately tell I wasn't doing too well. He showed up to my grandma's old crib back in St. Louis where I was hiding out at the time wanting to help but knew there was nothing he could really do until I was ready to accept it. So he left me to make a decision that somehow turned into all of this."

After my arrest for drug possession and subsequent banning from the league when I tested positive for the same drug, I wasn't expecting to ever be welcomed back onto these grounds; back into this city. But I was eternally grateful for Mr. Lloyd not only having a hand in my recovery, but also making my dream of coaching come true even if me being added to the staff made no sense to Selena.

Or maybe it did make sense to her, an astonished look on her face when she gushed, "Wow, Dre. I had no idea."

"You wouldn't. Ain't exactly my favorite thing to talk about," I told her, knowing the Lloyd family and some of my old teammates from the Trojans were the only people who really knew the full truth.

Now that shortlist included her, something I had a

feeling I wouldn't regret once she smiled and insisted, "It's super inspiring, though."

Instead of fully agreeing, I shrugged. "Yeah, maybe one day it will be. But right now, it's still too fresh for me to know if there's truly a happy ending or not."

Of course I wanted there to be a happy ending. Really, I *needed* there to be a happy ending since I wasn't sure what I would do otherwise. But for the meantime, I was taking it day-by-day; though it was clear Selena saw things in a more positive light when she offered, "I think there will be."

Naturally, my eyebrow piqued in surprise at her vote of confidence. "Oh yeah? How you figure?"

"Cause you're here with us, and we got you," she suggested with a look that begged for me to believe her.

I *wanted* to believe her. But I also had hard evidence telling me not to get too ahead of myself, a smirk on my lips when I reminded her, "Couple days ago you ain't wanna have shit to do with me, Selena."

Grabbing my hand, she gave it a squeeze to emphasize, "Well I do now, Dre. I get it now."

"And I appreciate that," I replied, squeezing her hand right back. And then we just sat there, *hand-in-hand*, trying to figure out how the hell we'd gotten here.

At least, that's what I was thinking, already smacking myself for digging the vibe between us so much as Selena finally snatched her hand away to say, "I... should probably go get in the cold tub right quick so I'm not dragging at practice tomorrow."

With a nod, I stood up to agree. "Yeah, can't have you blamin' me when your ass is back to brickin' again. I tried to save you, lil' baby."

Giggling, she stood up and matched my stance toe-to-toe. "Nah, you tried to play me. And that's something I don't take kindly."

"It won't happen again, Ms. Samuels," I assured, quickly finding myself caught up in the moment of *just...* being with her as I stared down into her eyes waiting for her to make a move.

When she slowly licked her lips, I assumed she felt it too. But instead of doing anything about it - *and probably doing us both a favor* - she gave me a little pat to my chest and said, "Have a good rest of your day, Dre."

FIVE

GAME DAY.

I almost couldn't believe it was here, couldn't believe that I was actually getting ready to begin my fourth season as a professional in the league I'd dreamed about since I was a little girl. Granted, early on, some of that dream was force-fed by my father who did everything he could to turn me into the athlete he wished my older brother was still alive to be. But now, it was totally mine, and I was grateful for the opportunity to play the game I loved most at the highest level it could be played, lacing up my kicks as Coach Sugar approached me with a grin.

"How many you got for me tonight, Sharpie?" she asked, somehow making a nickname out of my nick-name in only a way she could.

"However many it takes for us to get this win, Coach," I answered confidently, ready to set the tone for the season and put my team on the radar as a viable contender for the championship.

Not that people thought our squad was trash. I mean, making it to the playoffs in our inaugural season last year was certainly nothing to sneeze at. But because Nashville wasn't considered a big market, we didn't get the same media coverage as some of the other top teams which automatically put us at a disadvantage; something I knew would only change if we gave them a reason to watch us.

I'm going *to give them a reason to watch us.*

"I like the sound of that," Sugar finally responded with a nod, moving her hands to her pockets as she continued, "Dre told me he's been putting in some extra work with you and that three-pointer. I'm looking forward to seeing the results."

"Me and you both," I replied shortly, knowing that was the most I could say on it without letting my feelings about that "extra work" ruin the competitive edge I had worked up.

I mean, hating Dre was easy when he was just my former favorite player who blew his chances at glory, making him undeserving of an opportunity like this. But now that I knew the backstory of his downfall, I not only felt bad for talking shit about him, I also admired the fact that he was fully committed to bouncing back which was exactly why I couldn't talk about it since, *well*, it made me feel all warm, and fuzzy, and soft when I thought about the conversations we'd shared surrounding that particular topic.

He was so open, and honest, and genuinely nice as fuck while also somehow maintaining his grit and being fine as hell. And he understood the game like no other, dropping gems during each of our extended practices that only made me take to him even more since I'd never been around a guy who knew more than I did about basketball.

Okay, maybe that was a stretch. But he knew a lot, and it was refreshing to be able to learn from someone, to follow instead of lead, to be pushed instead of relying solely on self-motivation, *to…*

"Y'all *were* only working on jumpshots, right?" Sugar asked, her question interrupting the thoughts I was supposed to be avoiding in the first place.

Thinking back on her question, I realized I must've been in *extra* deep, trying to play it off when I frowned and asked, "Are you asking me what I think you're asking me, Coach Daniels?"

Instead of clarifying, she only smirked and shrugged. "Just checking the temperature, Selena."

"Just checking the temperature," I repeated with a chuckle, giving my most convincing grin when I told her, "Dre's a great basketball coach. And that's the only thing I know him as."

I expected that to be the answer she wanted to hear, especially since it was the truth; *for now.* But the frown she responded with had me confused until she groaned, "*Hmph.* That's unfortunate."

"Oh my God…" I sighed with another chuckle, getting ready to call her out on her comment until the culprit himself approached, bringing an immediate smile to Sugar's lips as she looked up at him to gush, "*Dre.* We were just talking about you."

His eyebrow piqued like he was surprised to hear it. "Oh yeah? I hope it was all good things."

"Of course it was," Sugar practically sang, directing her attention towards me to say,

"Selena will get you up to speed. I need to finish making my rounds."

In what felt like a blink of an eye, she was already a

few locker spots down, making a guest appearance in the background of one of Mikayla's annoying ass *Instagram* videos that had me rolling my eyes until Dre said, "So… catch me up."

With a wave of my hand, I bent over in my seat to double-check my laces as I told him, "It was nothing, really. I was just telling Sugar that you're a great coach. There's not a lot of people who can push me and get away with it, not a lot of people that I trust to make me a better ball player. But *you*… you've done that. And I don't exactly hate you for it."

That rumbling chuckle of his was enough to grab my full attention, prompting me to sit back up as he replied, "You got a funny way of giving compliments, Selena. But I'll take it. I mean, I guess you weren't lying about looking forward to those... hands-on lessons."

The way he said it had me shifting in my seat, my head cocked when I pursed my lips together and asked, "*Hm?*"

"In your media day interview. You said you'd learned from my example and felt lucky to now have access to more hands-on lessons like the work we've been putting in," he reminded me, the fact that he was really only repeating my words back to me not bringing me nearly enough relief since they took a totally different tone coming from his lips.

Still, I did my best to play it off yet again, letting out an airy, "Oh, right. *Those* kinda hands-on lessons."

Like he could read my mind, he chuckled again. "Come on, lil' baby. Get your head outta the gutter."

"It's not!" I quickly defended, my cheeks growing warm as I lied, "I just… forgot I said that."

"*Mmhmm.* You ready to ball out tonight?" he asked,

changing the subject to what should've been the sole thing on my mind. But now, it was sharing space with thoughts of what Dre could do with those extra large, tattoo-covered hands of his, my mouth watering at the thought of him palming my ass like a basketball, and… *shit*.

Nodding, I did my best to shake it off. "Balling out is the only reason I'm here, Coach Leonard."

From the pleased look on his face, I assumed my answer was sufficient. Though I couldn't miss the boyish grin that followed when he commented, "My first time seeing The Sharpshooter live in action. Shit, I'm lowkey excited."

"Uh, it's your first game coaching, Dre. You should be excited about that."

"I'm excited about both, Selena. *Equally* excited," he emphasized with a lick of his lips like he was trying to make a point.

The exact kind of point that had the power to get us both in trouble, prompting me to pop up from my chair and warn, "Go on somewhere with the flattery before Sugar asks me if we're fuckin' again."

"*Again?*" he asked, his shock making me giggle as I gave him a little pat to the chest to tell him, "And *now* you're up to speed. See you out on the court, Coach."

Before he could respond, I was already on my way out of the locker room, giving daps to a few of the arena staff members that I passed on the path to the court that immediately put things back into perspective the second I stepped on it.

This was what I was here for.

This was what it was all about.

This was home.

And it was time to show everybody we were on a serious mission this season, my eyes tightening as I started to lock in until I heard someone say, "Mama, there goes that *wo*-man!"

Peeking over, I honestly hated the way a grin came to my lips once I noticed what he was wearing, surely giving him the wrong impression that I was happy to see him sitting courtside when really I was just happy to see his attire.

Gnawing on my lip in an effort to hide some of that excitement, I commented, "Nice jersey, Kage."

"You know I had to show love," he replied with a smile of his own, adjusting his replica of my Nymphs number twenty jersey over his lanky frame before insisting, "Now come on. Let me get one for the 'gram right quick."

"One for the 'gram" turned into what felt like a mini-photoshoot, Kage hitting all types of goofy poses that had me cracking up laughing by the time we were done. But my laugh got caught in my throat when I saw Dre hiding out in the tunnel with Kat who was happily adjusting the front of his suit jacket before smoothing it over his chest, looking every bit of a proud girlfriend as they chatted about... *whatever.*

It didn't matter.

It was none of my business.

And because it was none of my business, I focused on what *was* my business, smiling for a few more professional pictures with Kage before getting back on the court for warm-ups.

"First game ball of the season goes to none other than Ms. Sharp-shooter herself for shooting an impressive six-for-eight from behind the arc and leading us to victory."

The locker room went up in celebration, a few of my teammates crowding over me to show extra love as Mikayla caught it all on video through her front-facing camera. Typically, I'd be annoyed about it. But today, I didn't mind since a solid four of those six three-pointers came off incredible assists from her, encouraging me to hop in the background of her recording to say, "Shoutout to my point guard!"

That only made things even more boisterous, Sugar laughing right along with us before urging, "Alright, alright. Settle down. The faster we finish, the faster y'all can get to postgame, and the faster y'all can get outta here!"

Knowing that was the ultimate motivator to get us to do anything, we found comfortable spots to receive the rest of Sugar's message before she dismissed us to get cleaned up for postgame interviews. And while I thought nothing of pulling my damp jersey off right there in the middle of the locker room, catching Dre's eyes on me from across the room made me feel especially naked as I turned to face the locker like that somehow changed things.

I mean, it wasn't his first time seeing me in just my sports bra and shorts, so it shouldn't have been a big deal. But now that I had gotten to know him a little better, my attraction to him had grown substantially, his attention making my heart race as I peeked over my shoulder to find him heading my way.

Leaning against the empty wall space next to me, he

commented, "Game ball, huh? Congratulations. Much deserved."

"You want it? I have enough of these at home already," I offered teasingly as I put on a t-shirt so that I could actually face him without feeling exposed.

It didn't make much of a difference though, Dre's ogling only intensifying when he replied, "Superstar shit. I bet your mama is real proud."

If there was anything to dim the excitement of the moment, it was that, my entire demeanor turning somber as I quietly agreed, "She would be, I'm sure."

That was the most I could say without giving a full explanation. Though from the look on Dre's face, I could tell that's what he was expecting, probably because he had been so open about his family history with me.

I couldn't do that, though.

Not here, and definitely not right now, grateful for Mikayla's interruption when she came over towards my locker singing, "Okay, Sharpshooter! I see you on your cougar shit."

"Cougar shit?" I asked with a frown, glancing down at the phone she was already shoving into my hands to show me what was she talking about. And all it took was a tiny peek for me to defend, "That is *not* what it looks like."

Taking a closer view, I almost couldn't believe how cozy Kage and I looked as we laughed about whatever silly comment he'd made in the moment. But I knew it was the caption of a heart and a basketball emoji that really put the cherry on top, Mikayla putting things even more into perspective once she replied, "You know the truth doesn't matter. People are already having a field day in the comments; crowning y'all as the king and queen of Nashville and everything."

The fact that people were so quick to jump to conclusions had me hot, and Dre only added to that when he chimed in, "Cute. Real cute," before leaving us to deal with the situation. Or rather, leaving me to deal with the situation since Mikayla was more entertained by the in-person tension, a grin on her face as she whistled, "Whew. Juggling *two* fine ass niggas. As if I needed another reason to look up to you…"

Once again, I found myself on the defense when I whined, "I'm not juggling anybody."

"That heart on IG from Kage and that shady ass comment from Coach in response to it says otherwise," Mikayla insisted, earning a mean side eye that had her holding her hands up to add, "But, hey. If you say you're not juggling, then you're not juggling. No beef this way."

Flashbacks of that cheapshot I gave her in practice must've ran through her head with how quick she was to make her position clear. But really, I couldn't blame her for noticing that Dre and I had taken an interest in each other while Kage had taken advantage of yet another public opportunity to shoot his shot; a shot I knew I had to work in my favor by taking one for the team.

Grabbing my own phone, I logged into *Instagram* and was hit with a ridiculous number of notifications; from likes, to new followers, and everything in between. But it only took a few scrolls past more recently posted pictures for me to find what I was looking for, giving the post of Kage and I a quick double-tap to "like" it before finally making my way to the postgame press conference.

SIX

COMFORTABLE OUTFIT, neck pillow, snacks, a couple episodes of my favorite sports podcast The Zone downloaded to my phone...

I had everything I needed, and somehow it still didn't feel like enough to keep me calm for the roughly two-and-a-half-hour flight to Connecticut for the Nymphs' first away game. Now that the season was in full swing, it was inevitable that we'd be taking flights pretty frequently. But because we had been spoiled with our first three games of the season being at home - *and had been busily focused on that* - I hadn't really had a chance to get mentally prepared for this part of the deal.

Yeah, flying had never been my thing, partly due to my grandmother's fear of plane crashes that she passed down to me. And it certainly didn't help that in this league, they flew commercial instead of chartering private planes the way we'd done back when I was a player which meant we had to share it with a bunch of other unpredictable people.

And babies.

Fuck.

Handing over my ticket to the gate agent, I lowkey wished the machine would deny me so I'd be given a pass to just find a bus or train to take instead. But when it beeped in approval, I realized it was time for me to face my fate, doing a slow stroll down the jetbridge onto the plane and into the row that only included me for now.

"Anybody but a baby," I thought with a quick glance at the empty seat next to me, pushing my bag of supplies under the seat in front of me as I heard someone from the aisle say, "I see the universe is tryna be funny."

Peeking up, I found Selena scooting into the seat next to mine to let others get past her before asking, "You mind if I take the window?"

"Prefer it actually. Ain't shit out there I'm tryna see once we take off," I answered, standing up to follow her lead out into the aisle so that we could switch seats more efficiently. And during that transition, I caught a wink from Sugar who was sitting in the very first row; a wink that had me a little confused as I sat down in my new seat just in time to hear Selena's response.

"Taking off is the best part, Dre. I mean, when else do you get to soar above it all like this?"

"Soar above a bunch of shit we can crash right on into if something goes wrong? Nah, I'm good on that, lil' baby," I replied with a chuckle that wasn't all that humorous since crashing into something was all I could really think about right now.

Well, that and the fact that Selena's bun of braids was sitting adorably crooked on the top of her head when she cocked it to ask, "How is it even possible for you to have played in the league for years, played college for a year, *and* gone all the way overseas to hoop, but still be afraid of flying?"

Thinking of it that simply, of course it sounded silly. But unfortunately, the truth was a little more complicated than that; though I didn't shy away from admitting, "Back then, I could pop a xannie and just sleep the whole way. But, *for obvious reasons*, that's no longer an option."

I could tell my explanation caught her a bit off-guard, but she didn't jump to judgment, nodding along before pulling one of her *AirPods* from her ear and offering it to me.

"*Here.* Listen to this. I think it might make this whole flying thing a little easier for you."

While I could appreciate her trying to help me out, my face still scrunched teasingly when I groaned, "*Ew.* I don't know where your ears been."

Making a smacking noise with the back of her teeth, she challenged, "Do you wanna have a smoother flight or not, negro?"

After a brief moment of deliberation, I accepted the earbud, holding it near my ear instead of sticking it in just to fuck with her. But that was enough for her press play on whatever it was she wanted me to listen to which turned out to be not at all what I was expecting.

"Selena, you know I got mad respect for you. But what the fuck is this honky tonk bullshit?" I asked, struggling to hold in my laugh as the flight attendant strolled past to check that we had our seatbelts fastened.

"The song is not even twenty seconds in, Dre," she whined like what was beyond the intro was any better. And because it only got more and more country the longer she let it play, I really started laughing as I quietly acknowledged, *"Got banjos in the background and shit…"*

That made her press pause. *"See.* I try to be nice and help you through this, but you playin'."

"Nah, *you* playin'. Tryna have a nigga out here on his yee-haw shit this Summer. Your Nashville upbringing is showin' big time," I teased with more laughter, making her roll her eyes as she pressed play to let the song finish. And once it was over, I handed her *AirPod* back as I concluded, "I mean, shorty can blow. I'll give you that. But I don't know if you'd ever catch me joining in on the line dance to this shit."

Now she was the one giggling. "I can't see you joining in on the line dance for anything, Dre."

"Man, what? Ya' boy will get low to the flo' on the Cha-Cha slide."

Like she was legitimately surprised to hear it, her eyebrow piqued when she asked, "Your old man knees really allow for that kinda activity?"

"Wowwww. You got jokes."

"You tried to clown my girl Jayde's EP. It's only right I get you back," she defended like I didn't have my reasons. And really, I hadn't even clowned the singer, just the old country song choice that Selena, *for whatever reason,* thought would calm me down.

"I guess the humor of it all did some good," I decided in my head as I reminded Selena, "I said she can sing. It just ain't my type of vibe, that's all."

"Okay, so what *is* your vibe then? I mean, being from St. Louis, who y'all got? Nelly and the St. Lunatics? Chingy?" she listed with a hint of sarcasm in her tone like she was trying to use the Midwest legends to clown me.

I wasn't offended though since I knew they all had hits, an easy smile on my lips when I challenged, "Don't act like they ain't have your ass hittin' the chickenhead back in the day."

Smirking, she quickly replied, "I didn't say that. Those are just the only artists I know from the area."

"So the Sharpshooter was in her lil' school dances fuckin' it up, huh?" I teased, doing a mini-rendition of the dance in my seat that had Selena cracking up laughing before she corrected me.

"Nah, the Sharpshooter skipped school dances in favor of going to the gym."

"Somehow, that doesn't surprise me," I commented, the slight frown on her face in response giving way to my explanation. "Because of your work ethic. I can tell it's been in you for a long ass time by how hard you go."

Even though it didn't bring her smile back completely, she did nod along to agree with me before going into a little explanation of her own. "I graduated from high school early so that I could get to Lynstone and start training at a collegiate level. Then I didn't walk in my graduation from Lynstone so that I could be present for my first training camp as a professional out in LA after I got drafted. I've dumped boyfriends, canceled vacations, and didn't meet my youngest baby brother until he was like seven-months-old because of '*how hard I go*'. So really, my work ethic *is*… kinda problematic."

Now I was the one doing a slow nod. "If you feel like you've missed out, I could see why you'd say that. But your work ethic is also what got you here, so maybe it was worth something."

"All that hard work just to be sitting here on a plane

with you. *Oh yeah*. Totally worth it," she replied sarcastically with a half-hearted smile, peeking back out of the window before she added, "But, hey. We got you in the air without you having a panic attack. So I guess my job here is done."

Once she mentioned it, I was honestly kind of shook that I hadn't noticed we'd already taken off, so focused on her that nothing else going on really mattered. But considering this was one of the rare times we could be in each other's faces without it seeming suspicious, I decided to take full advantage when I asked, "Does it have to be?"

Of course, if she wanted to relax, listen to her little country jams and be in her own world, I wasn't going to bother her. But to be real, I just enjoyed talking to her, *getting to know her*. And thankfully that feeling seemed to be mutual according to the way Selena smiled before posing a question of her own.

"Tell me something I don't know about you, DeAndre Leonard."

"Well for starters, my real first name isn't DeAndre."

If it weren't for her seatbelt, Selena would've hit her head on the flight attendant call button at that, a look of disbelief on her face when she squealed, "Excuse me, what?!"

With my hands, I urged, "*Chill, chill*. This is top secret information."

"*Clearly*. I mean, I know a lot about you. Like, a lot a lot. And that's not something I've *ever* come across in my *Google* searches."

"Damn, Selena. Searches plural? You know you could've just asked me whatever you wanted to know, right?" I pressed, taking great pleasure in watching her get flustered about it even though I was teasing her.

"It was a long time ago! Before I knew you," she defended, settling down to ask, "But anyway, what's your real first name?"

"Jordan."

I don't know what she was expecting, but somehow the name on my birth certificate must not have been it considering the way her head snapped back when she repeated, "*Jordan?* Seriously?"

"Yeah, for real. Jordan DeAndre Leonard."

Her confused expression remained. "So why do you go by DeAndre instead of Jordan?"

Releasing a short sigh, I explained, "I've always known I wanted to play ball on the biggest stage since I was a kid. But as far as basketball personas went, Jordan was already taken. So I decided to create my own with my middle name."

I expected my explanation to relieve her confusion, but her eyes only seemed to tighten even more when she asked, "You really abandoned your first name because of Michael Jeffrey Jordan?"

Chuckling, I replied, "Abandoned is a strong word. And it ain't all that uncommon. I mean, people rarely call Magic, Earvin. And they damn sure don't call Steph, Wardell. Hell, Kareem converted and made everybody forget he was first introduced to the basket-ball scene as Ferdinand."

That was enough for her to nod as she finally agreed, "All valid points. But also know, you'll forever be Jordan to me now."

She said it with the most adorable smile that would've had me going along with plenty more things in that moment had she asked. It was a total contrast to the fierceness she expressed on the court and whenever she felt passionate about something, creating the perfect balance that had me tempted to go against my own rule of keeping to myself.

Actually, I was already a step beyond tempted, licking my lips to reply, "When we're in private, I'll allow it."

Once the words flowed from my mouth, I knew I was putting myself at risk of causing trouble. But before I could cover with some bullshit explanation about her using it during our *"private"* shooting sessions, Selena bit down into her bottom lip and gushed, "Deal."

It was an unexpected but appreciated response that I immediately stored in the back of my mind for later, making a quick decision to break some of the tension between us by changing the subject since a plane of mixed company wasn't the place for that kind of conversation.

"Aight, I gave you somethin' juicy. Now tell me about you."

Releasing a little sigh of her own, she started, "*Well...* I told you I have a baby brother. He's technically my half-brother; one of many new siblings that came as a result of my father remarrying right after I graduated high school."

"So your parents are divorced?"

"Actually, my mother passed away when I was young," she quietly explained, pursing her lips together to swallow down her emotions about it that had me feeling bad for even asking.

"Sorry to hear that."

She only shrugged as she continued, "Yeah, so it was

just me and my dad until he met... *her*. And now they have their own little family together."

There was an edge to her tone that gave additional context, something I was sure to comment on when I inquired, "I take it you're not all that happy about it?"

Again, she shrugged. "I'm happy he's happy. But I'm not happy about what our relationship has turned into because of it. I mean, with the sudden loss of my mother and big brother, we became really tight out of necessity. We were all each other had, you know? But now, things are just... *different*."

There was a lot to her response, but the only thing I could focus on was, "*Wait.* So you said you lost a brother too?"

With a wry smile, she replied, "Gained an angel, yeah. Him and my mom got into a really bad car accident on the way to one of his basketball practices. Neither of them were wearing their seatbelts."

"*Damn.* Were you close with your brother? I mean, with y'all both being hoopers?"

Even though I knew nothing about him, somehow I could already envision him and Selena hooping in their driveway as kids, playing one-on-one until dinnertime or until the street lights came on. I could see Selena being invited into the competitive neighborhood hoop sessions thanks to her big brother's clout, or hell, maybe even the other way around. And I couldn't even begin to imagine how she felt losing what should've been a forever teammate, wondering if those were the kind of memories playing in her head when she finally answered, "I'd say we were as close as a preteen basketball fanatic could be to his doll-obsessed kindergarten sister. We didn't always get along. But he was my protector, and I loved him for it."

Taking a pause, she then continued, "Surprisingly enough, I didn't really start playing basketball until after he passed. One of my father's favorite things to do was to watch Scottie hoop. They'd talk about what blue-blood college he was going to ball for, where he was going to play professionally, even what his first basketball shoe design would look like. But after the accident, my father became deeply depressed knowing none of that would ever be. So I thought maybe if I picked up a ball, he'd feel better."

I didn't think it was possible. But now that I knew where her love for the game came from, I respected her commitment to the craft even more. I mean, not only did she play to help her father be able to feel again, but she played to honor her brother's memory, to see his dreams through. And that was commendable on so many levels, something that was hard to find the words to express when I replied, "Wow. *That's...*"

"Deep as hell for someone who was like five or six at the time?" she interrupted with a little chuckle. "Yeah, it's crazy. But it became our thing. Everything he wanted for Scottie, all the energy he was putting into making Scottie's hoop dreams come true, he invested in me. And that's how I became the basketball lunatic I am today."

"The basketball *superstar* you are today," I corrected, falling a little more in like with her signature smile when she served it and agreed, "Yeah, that too."

"Sorry for being all in your business. I'm sure that's not easy to talk about."

Shaking her head, she sighed. "No, it's not. And I

rarely, I mean *rarely*, get this personal. *But…* it felt good to get that out. So thank you."

Knowing she'd opened up a little more than she normally would lowkey had me feeling special, reaching for her hand and giving it a squeeze as I told her, "Anytime, Selena."

"*SeSa.* That's what my mother used to call me. Another fun fact for your Selena Samuels file," she offered with a smile that had me cheesing too.

"Country-music listening, chickenhead-champion, Selena "SeSa" Samuels. *Wait.* SeSa, because *Se*-lena and…"

"*Ding, ding, ding.* You got it. So brilliant," she gushed sarcastically, making me drop her hand with a playful side eye as I groaned, "I see your compliment game is still trash."

Smirking, she replied, "I stroke three-pointers, not egos."

"Shit, you barely do that," I teased, dodging her little jab to my arm as I held up my hands to tell her, "I'm playin', I'm playin'. Your Sharpshooter nickname is *beyond* fitting. But you know I'm bouta play that SeSa shit out now, right?"

"I'd be disappointed if you didn't. I mean, what's the point of knowing top secret info like that if you aren't gonna use it to tease me, Jordan?" she asked so effortlessly that I almost forgot no one called me that shit anymore.

But because I'd already warned her about keeping that on the low, I now had an excuse to get a little more into her personal space to whisper, "*Shhh.* You way too loud, SeSa."

Scrunching closer to the window to create some space between us, she giggled, "You're so annoying."

"You like it."

She didn't confirm or deny my claim, only smirked as she dramatically slipped her *AirPod* back into her ear to signal our conversation was over. And I thought I'd be good with that until I started digging into my bag for my own headphones and couldn't find them.

Shit.

The panic of not having something to keep me occupied for the rest of the flight quickly started to settle in and my search became even more urgent, Selena taking notice enough to tease, "You know… you could always listen to more Jayde with me."

"Nah, I left my cowboy boots at home," I replied as I continued digging, only making her giggle again before she explained, "It's not all country, Dre. The other half is like, 2000's R&B. I know you can get with that."

That was enough for me to give her offer some consideration, mainly off the strength of trying to understand how a project with both genres even made sense. And as I checked a few last spots in my bag - *and came up empty-handed* - I acknowledged, "That's quite the combination."

"What can I say? Her voice sounds bomb no matter what she's singing."

Now that it seemed like I didn't have much of a choice if I planned on surviving this thing, I accepted the *AirPod* she had dangling my way, wiping it clean on my sweatshirt before putting it in my ear. Then I closed my eyes in an attempt to force myself to sleep; though all I saw on the other side of my eyelids were visions of Selena's pretty ass.

That smile, those braids, that… *fire*.

She was everything I wanted and everything I couldn't have all at once, knowing getting myself involved with her meant putting the rest of my world in jeopardy. I mean, this job was still pretty new, and the one request I had from my boss was to leave Selena alone. But here she was anyway, and here I was, relishing in what felt like a real friendship ripe with the potential for something greater; something worth the risk.

Honestly, that was the wildest part of it all. The fact that I was finally on the rebound both personally and professionally but was willing to put that in danger for a chance with her. Then again, what was the worst that could happen?

Since I had nothing but time to really think this whole thing through, I decided to start weighing the pros and cons. At least, that's what I thought I was doing until I heard Selena say, "*Dre*. Dre, we're here."

My eyes were slow to open, first squinting against the cabin lights that had been turned back on and then to the people around us who were all already busy with their phones now that we'd apparently landed.

Stretching in my seat as much as I could, I groaned, "*Damn*. I don't even remember fallin' asleep."

"One minute you were humming along to one of Jayde's covers and the next you were out cold tryna cuddle up on me," Selena replied with a teasing smirk that made it hard for me to tell if she was being truthful or not.

Either way, I had no problem doing a little teasing of my own when I told her, "You should've let me. I've heard I'm good at it."

The reaction I expected wasn't the reaction I received, a slight frown on Selena's face as she asked, "*I...* who told you that? Someone who wanted your money? Cause I imagine cuddling with you being similar to cuddling with one of those science class skeletons."

Because it was a good joke, we both started laughing as I moved to tickle her and playfully growled, "You got me fucked up."

From the way she was practically wheezing, I knew her being ticklish as hell was another fact for me to add to my file on her; airy laughs that only encouraged me to keep going until I heard Mikayla say, "*Geez*. Get a room, you two."

Since the last thing I needed was for her nosy ass to start livestreaming this little interaction to her followers, I pulled back, Selena still giggling as she whined, "See. You're gonna get us in trouble."

"Shouldn't have been talkin' shit," I told her with a shrug, grabbing my bag to deboard the plane with Selena right behind me still joking around.

"At least you're a fine ass skeleton," she squealed once she caught up with my strides towards baggage claim, surely so she could see the reaction on my face to what was, *yet again*, another wack ass compliment.

Shaking my head with a grin, I didn't even look her way to reply, "I'm done talkin' to you, Selena."

"*Awww*. So you mad, huh?"

Again, I shook my head. "Nah, we all about body positivity over this way. I love myself," I told her, pulling up the hem of my t-shirt to do a slow rub of my abs that had Selena biting into her lip as she checked me out.

In fact, she was staring so hard that she almost got

ran over from behind by one of those airport golf carts, the loud honk it gave embarrassing the fuck out of her as she jumped out of the way then held up her hand to yell, "Sorry!"

Now I was the one laughing at her, waiting until she returned to my side to tell her, "See. Karma for all that shit talkin'."

Snapping her head back, she gushed, "*Wow*. My life was in danger and that's how you do me?"

"Ain't like I would've been able to stop it with my skeleton body anyway," I replied with a shrug that had Selena right back on her teasing tangent as she wrapped herself around my arm and started singing, *"Feelings. So deep in his feelings."*

Honestly, with her being so close and our banter flowing so easily, I kind of forgot we had an audience until Kat stepped in front of us with her arms crossed to ask, "Dre, can I speak to you for a minute?"

Even though we really weren't doing anything wrong, Selena was still quick to remove herself from the situation, mouthing a, *"Sorry,"* with her exit towards where the rest of the team had congregated around the baggage carousel as I gave a casual, "What's up?"

Kat was wearing a smile, but her tone was still sharp when she asked, "Care to tell me what that was all about? Cause I'm pretty sure I made myself clear about you two staying away from each other."

I would've been lying if I didn't admit, *at least to myself*, that her concerns were valid. My feelings for Selena were starting to show their ass no matter how deep I tried to bury them. But since the last thing I needed was for Kat to grow more suspicious before I even knew how Selena truly felt about me, I did my best to play it down.

"She's my player. We're friends. It's really not that deep."

Instead of accepting my response, Kat stepped closer to advise, "Look, Dre. I get it. Selena's pretty, she's charismatic, she's all that and more. But part of keeping her focused on that championship is keeping her hungry, and I can't have her getting full off your attention."

Something about her words didn't sit right with me, a frown on my face when I asked, "*Wait*. So first it was a PR thing, and now it's about a championship? I mean, you do realize I'm not the only nigga in Nashville, right? She could be getting *"full"* regardless of what you think we got goin' on."

Shaking her head, she reasoned more to herself than me, "Nah. Now that we're in season, I doubt she has the time to start something fresh. Then again, I *have* noticed something brewing between her and Kage, so maybe I need to check his little ass too."

To a regular person, it probably sounded crazy. But I knew some of these owners would do whatever to get that trophy and the clout that came with it, going as far as inserting themselves into the personal lives of their players if they knew it could have an effect on the outcome. And considering who Kat's father was, and the fact that she'd watched him wheel and deal in the same position for over a decade with the Trojans, I wasn't surprised that she'd inherited the gene.

Still, that didn't mean I was going to let her overregulate my moves with that shit, placing a hand to her shoulder to give a little advice of my own. "Do what you gotta do. But just know, I'm here to do my job and that's all."

From the look in her eyes, I knew she wanted to believe me. But she didn't back down from her position, smirking to suggest, "Well I'm gonna need you in the mirror repeating that shit like an affirmation every time you think about fuckin' around with our shooting guard, okay?"

No lie, hearing it out loud made it hit a little different, thinking back on that pros and cons list I was supposed to make before I fell asleep on the plane. And since pissing off my boss was definitely a top con, I made a quick decision to fall back for now, softening her a little bit when I sweetly answered, "Sure thing, Katianna."

Her smirk remained for a beat longer than necessary before she moved onto something else. And when I finally did the same, it was only to catch the unreadable look on Selena's face as she caught my eyes for a split second before rushing to pull them away.

SEVEN

THE BALL WAS in my hands, and I knew exactly what I was going to do with it.

First, an inbounds pass to Mikayla at half court. Then, set up my defender to get checked with a back screen from Talia so that I could get in position for Mikayla's pass back to me for a corner three-pointer to win the game.

It was a simple play; one we had drilled repeatedly in practice and even walked through just earlier this morning for situations like this. And I was more than ready to make it happen, more than ready to accept yet another game ball for leading us to victory as I watched Mikayla blow past her defender to create enough space so that she could get a clean pass off to me.

Except... it wasn't a clean pass; the defender using every inch of her wingspan to catch just enough of the ball with her fingertips and deflect it in a way that had me scrambling to both secure the ball and get a shot up before the buzzer went off. And from there, it felt like everything was going in slow motion, the ball rotating through the air - *and only ever touching air* - as the other team secured it near the rim with time already expired to win the game.

Watching our opponents celebrate surviving a close one on their home court came second to my personal scolding, trying to figure out how I'd missed so badly. I mean, sure I was drained from playing damn near the entire game because of how competitive it was from start to finish. But I lived for moments like this; *I showed up for moments like this*. And I'd shot well all game, making this fluke of an air ball even harder to understand.

With a frustrated clap, I finally headed towards our bench, not at all soothed by the, *"My fault"* Mikayla expressed in reference to her sketchy pass, or the, *"That's alright, Sharpie"* Coach Sugar offered with a pat to my shoulder, or the optimistic, *"You'll hit it next time"* from Dre like he knew there'd be one. Even as we slapped hands with the other team, all I could think about was the shot.

No rim.

No net.

No backboard.

All air.

Soaring close enough to the target for everyone to know it was a legitimate attempt, and I blew it.

Fuck.

When their head coach stopped me for a quick conversation, I was hardly present enough to catch any of her words, only nodding along until she gave me the customary back pat to signal she was done. And as I made my way towards the locker room, I threw a towel over my head and kept my eyes low, knowing any eye contact would turn into an autograph request I wasn't in the mood to sign or a picture I didn't want to take.

Not today.

Not after… that.

What the fuck was that, Selena?

As Coach Sugar gave her postgame remarks, the question played over and over again in my head, even after she expressed how proud she was of us for fighting to the end and putting ourselves in position to win.

But we hadn't won.

There was no second-place winner in this shit; only a winner and a loser. And because of me, our season's record was no longer perfect, making the whole thing sting even more as we took the somber bus ride back to our hotel.

When we pulled up, I realized a few of our diehard fans were standing outside to welcome us, sending me through another blitz of what was supposed to be encouraging words for the rest of the season that really only reminded me of my fuck-up. And the frustration of that followed me all the way to the room I was sharing with Talia who was already in the middle of a happy-go-lucky *FaceTime* call with her baby girl and partner back home like nothing had even happened.

For her, I suppose that was accurate since she'd done her job on that final play by getting me open. But as the one who hadn't delivered, this shit sucked. And I wasn't sure what to do about it other than try to figure out what I'd done wrong.

Grabbing my iPad, I pulled up the clip that was already making its rounds on the internet under the headline, *"Connecticut Survives!"* when it really should've been, *"Selena Samuels Fails!"* watching it intently for any obvious errors. But unfortunately, the more I ran it back, the worse I felt about it, peeking over at Talia who was too busy cooing into the screen to notice my self-pity.

She did give me an idea though, one I wasted no time acting on as I hopped up from my bed to tell her, "I'll be back." And after catching the nod she gave my way to let me know she'd heard me, I grabbed my phone and left the room to make a *FaceTime* call of my own, waiting patiently with my back against the hallway wall for my father to pick up.

It rang for a while, to the point that I considered hanging up and going back to the room. But when the call finally connected, I was glad I hadn't, an instant grin on my lips when I caught the view of my father's chin because of the awkward way he had his phone positioned.

Yeah, he was still getting used to the technology. But at least he was there to hear my sighed, "Daddy."

"Selena. How are you, dear?" he asked, doing his best to adjust the screen to a better spot now that he could see how off he was.

But really, I just needed to hear his voice, needed to know he was there for me when I answered, "Not good. Did you see the game?"

"I caught the first few minutes. But baby boy was having trouble going to sleep, and I ended up putting the both of us down," he answered with a laugh that I wanted to join in on but struggled to since... *he really didn't watch my game?*

The answer to that question was clear when he followed up, "How'd you do?"

Pushing out another sigh, I replied, "*Uh*... well. Overall, I had a good game. But in the end, I..."

Before I could get to the most upsetting part, the

part I had really called to talk about, he cut me off. "*Gotdamnit.* Your brother is up and crying again. I think he's coming down with somethin'. Let me go check on him, and I'll give you a call back, okay?"

It shouldn't have been a big deal for him to call me back. Surely my needs weren't as urgent as the baby's, and my whining about the game could wait. But I also couldn't shake the disappointment of him rushing me off the phone. And maybe it was just my emotionally-vulnerable state, but admittedly I was upset when I told him, "Don't worry about it. I'll talk to you later," before ending the call without saying anything more.

Releasing another sigh, I rested against the wall with my eyes closed, squeezing my phone in my hand as I thought about who else I could rant to about the game. All of my teammates were out of the question since, *well*, they'd experienced the shit firsthand and were probably still mad at me for it. Ari would've been a no-brainer if she hadn't already texted me a note of support followed by a good night text that marked her as unavailable. And as far as my friends outside of the game went, I knew they wouldn't understand, leaving me with one last option.

Instead of making any assumptions, I opted to send him a text and was grateful for his almost immediate response.

"Hey. You around to chat?" - Selena

"Yeah. Room 1738." - Dre

Thankfully we were on the same floor, making it a quick trip to the other end of the long hallway that I put the hood of my jacket on for just in case some nosy folks - *mainly Mikayla* - were lurking around. And after a single knock, Dre pulled the door open, *notably shirtless*, moving to the side to let me past as he announced, "Excuse the mess. Tryna fit in my studies when I can."

"*Your studies*? You're back in school?" I asked once I saw the assortment of random papers, pens and highlighters, a textbook, and a laptop in the middle of his bed.

Shrugging, he plopped down onto the mattress and started straightening up while answering, "Just part-time, all online. Somethin' light."

He might've been playing humble about it, but I was too impressed to do the same when I pulled my hood down to tell him, "Still incredibly commendable, Dre. Especially while in-season."

"And because that was actually a decent compliment coming from you, I'll take it," he replied with a smile, patting the cleared space next to him as an invitation for me to take a seat.

Because I knew my intentions, I didn't hesitate to accept, not expecting to get goosebumps from his freshly-showered scent and the up-close view of the tattoos he was covered in. And when he asked, "What's on your mind?" in some especially sultry tone, I considered a different answer for a split second, doing my best to shake it off so that I could get to what I'd really come here for.

Pulling up the clip on my phone, I started, "Okay, so I've watched this final play back like a thousand times, and I can't see where I went so wrong. My mechanics were on point. The defender had just barely recovered from Talia's pick, so it wasn't like she was really in my way. And yeah, Mikayla's pass got tipped, but I still caught the ball."

When the clip started playing for a second time, Dre pressed paused and pointed to where I was positioned on the screen. "Selena, look where you shot it from."

"The three-point line. Exactly where I was supposed to be," I replied, not understanding his point until he pressed again.

"No. *Really* look where you shot it from," he repeated, my eyes squinted as he gave a full explanation. "Deep corner, damn near behind the hoop. Easily the hardest place to shoot from on the court, especially off-balance like you were when you landed after saving Mikayla's pass from going out of bounds."

He had a point, though I struggled to completely agree. "So it was a tough shot. That's still not an excuse for a fuckin' air ball."

"Can't make 'em all, lil' baby," he offered with a shrug that didn't exactly make me feel any better.

Well… his presence in general was somehow making me feel better, but not his words, a slight frown on my face when I told him, "I thought you'd have better advice than this."

For whatever reason, that made him chuckle as he stood up to reply, "I've played the game. I know how it goes. And yeah, those are the ones you wish you can get back, *but…* it happens, Selena. To all of us."

"In all that I've watched, I don't *ever* remember it happening to you," I challenged, watching as he rested against the edge of the dresser with a distant look that I wondered about until he quietly responded.

"Eleventh-grade. Class 5 state championship game. Wide-open fastbreak."

"*Oh no…*" I sighed, already feeling bad for bringing it up as he crossed his arms over his bare chest to explain, "Oh yeah. We were down one, whole crowd on their feet. I got a steal for a fastbreak and choked on the dunk that would've won us the state title for a third year in a row."

"*Dre…*" was all I could say, trying to imagine how his teen-self dealt with such a disappointing moment. Though when he rejoined me on the bed wearing a smirk, it seemed as if the whole thing was funny to him now; especially once he chuckled to say, "I know, right? Why didn't I just lay it up? How could I miss that? I dunked a solid four times in the game before that moment, so how did I trick-off the most important one? I had all those same questions. But the reality is, it happens. *Shit* happens."

"And that we both suck. Thanks for the show of solidarity," I told him teasingly, feeling a lot better about it now that I wasn't so… *alone.*

Not situationally, not emotionally, not physically. He was here with me in all of it, bumping his shoulder into mine when he groaned, "*Of everything your goofy ass could've gotten outta that story…*"

Giggling, I grabbed his hand to tell him, "No, seriously though. Thanks for that perspective. I've played a lot of games. I've missed plenty of shots. But never like that. Never for the game."

"And now you're in elite company because of it. Welcome to the club, Ms. Samuels," Dre offered, leaning my way to press a kiss against my forehead that made my cheeks flush warm. Then he bent a little lower to plant a soft kiss against the tip of my nose, my heart racing with anticipation of the inevitable next stop in his pattern that he unfortunately opted out of in favor of asking, "You feel better now?"

Because he was still so close, I only nodded my head *"yes"*, watching his lips curl into a grin when he replied, "*Good*. Cause I ain't want you to think I was tryna take advantage of you when I did this."

In what felt like one long blink, Dre's lips were on mine, kissing me so gently it was borderline infuriating since how could something so sweet and tender possibly have me feeling so hot?

When he cupped his hand against my chin, I understood. Dre had a lowkey sex appeal about him, a presence that didn't require him to do a bunch of extra shit to prove himself. He just delivered. He knew what he was doing. And when he slipped his tongue between my lips, I was giddy to receive his confidence, moaning as his hand gravitated towards the nape of my neck to pull me in even closer for a kiss I couldn't get enough of; for a moment I didn't want to end.

It *did* have to end, though. No matter how badly I wanted this kiss to carry into something more, I couldn't let it, Kat's message about keeping things professional playing in the back of my head as I pushed away with a groaned, "*Mm*. I should probably go. Let you get back to your studies."

Before he could even respond, I was already off the bed, rushing towards the door and getting it just barely cracked open when Dre snuck up behind me to push it back closed. Then he hovered near my ear and whispered, "*Stay*," my eyes fluttering shut once he pressed a lingering kiss against the side of my neck that made me forget why I was leaving in the first place.

I mean, his mouth was so skilled, knowing just the right spot to hit as I faltered, "But what about…"

"Stay, Selena," he requested in more of a growl, turning me around to press my back against the door then resting his forehead against mine. "I want you to stay."

The way he said it put the ball in my court, left with the decision to go with my mind and leave like I originally planned to, or go with my heart and… *fuck it.*

Wrapping my arms around his neck, I pulled his face down to mine for a kiss that was a lot more aggressive than before, filled with an urgency that led us back to his bed where I stumbled to straddle his lap as he unzipped my jacket and pushed it from my shoulders. Then he abandoned my lips in favor of my collarbone, nibbling into my skin with perfect pressure that had me grinding in his lap and singing his praises until he chuckled to remind me, "We gotta stay low. I got Sugar to the left of me and some of the medical staff on the right."

"Stop making me feel so good then," I halfway whined, only making Dre chuckle again.

"You don't want that."

"I *don't* want that," I agreed with a smirk that he matched to ask, "So what you want then, lil' baby?"

There was an innocent giddiness that was replaced with pure lust from hearing him call me that under these particular conditions, my hands pressed into his shoulders as I teasingly replied, "Somethin' I won't regret later."

Frowning, he asked, "You really think I'd waste your time like that?"

"*I mean...* you're wasting it now doin' all this talking, so..."

Without needing to say anything more, he flipped me onto my back, creating a trail of kisses from my neck, down my cleavage to my belly button where he lingered to pull my sweatpants down just enough to get to my panty line. Then he teased me with kisses from the left side to the right before standing up to rid me of my pants completely, my underwear of choice making it clear this was *not* on my agenda.

Dre wasn't fazed though, turning them into a total non-factor once I lifted my hips so that he could remove those too. But when he took a step away from the bed, I started to become a little concerned, wondering if he was having second thoughts until he quietly asked, "How the fuck was I supposed to resist you, Selena?"

The question had me flattered and turned on all at once; even more so as I watched him adjust the impressive erection struggling against the fabric of his basketball shorts before I answered, "The same way I was supposed to resist you. And yet, here I am."

"Yeah. Here you are," he groaned with a lick of his lips that gave me chills as he slowly rejoined me on the bed, this time positioning himself with his face between my thighs where he landed soft kisses against the inner part of each that had me damn near begging for him to stop torturing me.

Instead of giving me what I wanted, he only gave another reminder for me to, "*Shhh...*" pressing one of his abnormally long fingers against my lips as if that was all it would take for me to stay quiet once his tongue finally found its way to my clit for a taste that made my stomach clench and my lips part with a long exhale. And even that, he took full advantage of by slipping his finger into my mouth to pacify me, only turning me on even more as it became my way of showing my appreciation for how damn good his tongue felt as I sucked and moaned against it while he continued to devour me.

Peeking up at me with heated eyes, he warned, "Keep that shit up, and I'ma give you somethin' else to suck on," like that wasn't going to motivate me to do even more. In fact, I found myself issuing a challenge of my own when I scrapped it with my teeth, Dre watching me intently as he groaned, *"Hardheaded ass..."* before moving up the bed to kiss me with my flavor still lingering on his lips. Then he took the same finger that was in my mouth and slipped it between my wet folds, covering my moan with another kiss that I quickly found myself lost in as my senses became overwhelmed with pleasure now that I knew his hands were good for a lot more than just dribbling basketballs.

Honestly, Dre was just skilled all over; with his mouth, with his hands, with his intensity that straddled the line of just enough and too much for me to handle. And since I could pretty much assume that extended to his dick, I only grew wetter with anticipation, Dre taking notice as he used my arousal to rub circles against my clit while telling me, "This is the only thing I want you to remember about tonight, aight? Fuck that shot."

It took a second for me to realize what he was talking about, far too wrapped up in what he was doing to me to think about basketball at all. And even when it did come back to me, I didn't care nearly as much as I had when I first showed up to his room, fascinated by how easily Dre had been able to direct my attention elsewhere; at least for the moment.

Maybe later I'd go back to it. But right now, the only thing I was concerned about was how quickly I could get Dre inside of me, eager for something more than foreplay when I replied, "Shot forgotten. Now give me somethin' to remember."

For whatever reason, that made him chuckle as he moved away from the bed to get rid of his shorts, the way his dick jumped out when he tugged the waistband past his erection making me sit up onto my elbows for a better view that had him teasing, "Nah, you had jokes for us skinny niggas the other day. Don't be tryna show love now that you see I ain't slim all over."

Licking my lips, I would've been lying if I replied with anything other than, "I'll give you that." Though I also couldn't help doing a little teasing of my own when I added, "But I'm still not staying after to cuddle."

Breathing a low, *"hmph"* in response, he quickly fished a condom from his wallet sitting on the dresser, doing what was necessary to make sure we didn't have a slip-up before instructing me to turn my sexy ass over. And once I followed directions, he climbed onto the bed and unstrapped my bra, positioning himself to take me from behind in one long, gratifying stroke that had me arching my back and rushing to bury my face into the pillows all at once.

He didn't let me stay there though, knocking every pillow from my reach as he groaned, "Have some discipline, lil' baby. Hold that shit in." And I thought I was for sure going to combust when I breathily begged, *"Dre, please…"* his hands buried in my braids as he gave them a slight yank and growled, "Better not let them hear you, Selena. Don't get us caught."

The pressure was driving me crazy, only heightening

the experience as I struggled to stay quiet with every knock of his dick against my inner back wall. And he knew it too, moving us to a spoon position so that he could cover my mouth with his hand while he continued to fuck me into next season.

It was worth it, though. So damn worth it that I wanted to scream it loud for the entire hotel to hear. And when Dre moved his hand away from my mouth down to my clit, I considered taking my chances; though my thoughts were almost immediately drowned out by the extra stimulation that had my body buzzing with the telltale signs of an impending orgasm, my toes curled as Dre prolonged my climax with slow strokes that left me totally breathless.

Peppering kisses against my back as I came down from my high, I felt myself literally shiver when he pulled out and asked, "What I gotta do to make you feel better, lil' baby?"

Turning around to face him, I assured, "You've already done that, Dre."

I mean, if the mess between my thighs was any indication, he'd done that and more. Still, he shook his head, sitting up a little to disagree. "Nah. More than just that shot was sittin' heavy on your spirit when you came in here, I could tell. So what can I do about it?"

Thinking back to the circumstances surrounding my arrival, the details were a little foggy until I remembered the conversation - *or lack thereof* - with my father that led me here in the first place. And since I *definitely* wasn't going to let that blow my high, I quickly brushed him off. "It's nothin', really."

From the skeptical look on his face, I could tell he didn't believe me. But instead of pressing me for more info, he challenged, "Prove it," grinning mischievously as he pulled me on top to go another round. Or rather, wrap up his first round since only I'd made it to the finish line. And with that on my mind, I took his challenge even more personal, pressing into his chest for a lift until I noticed a woman's name tattooed in beautiful cursive right under my fingertips.

"*Wait.* Who's Eliza?"

The question came from a place of genuine interest, not making any assumptions or rushing to judgment about his past relationships. But when he answered, "Derives from the same place as the two names in that heart on your shoulder blade, Ms. Samuels," I realized how silly it was of me to bring it up at all, feeling like I'd ruined the mood until he lifted my chin to say, "Now quit gettin' distracted and ride me like ain't nothin' wrong with you."

It was an aggressive request, but one I was happy to fulfill, gliding down on top of his dick with a shared moan that gave me goosebumps as Dre growled, *"Got-damn."* And really, that was all I needed to hear to get back in the zone, taunting him the same way he did me when I leaned to whisper against his lips, "Better not let them hear you, Jordan."

EIGHT

SELENA SAMUELS WAS A FUCKIN' liar.

I could feel the ghost of my grandma's hand smacking me in the back of my head for even thinking that word - *liar, not fuckin'*. But it was the truth as I looked down at the beautiful face cuddled up against my chest, her body tightly snuggled under my arm and her leg draped over mine while she slept off an experience I'd left her no room to regret.

I mean, would she regret how tired she'd more than likely be during our walkthrough practice in New York later this evening because of this? *Probably.* But other than that, there wasn't a single moment she could classify as not worth it, something I'd made sure of since facing her for the rest of the season would've been embarrassing as hell otherwise.

It wasn't *all* about my ego, though. There was an easy connection between Selena and I, an attraction that I was tired of trying to shake solely because of our circumstances. Sure, they weren't ideal and had the potential to cause a bit of a stir if - *when* - people found out about us. But I was really supposed to ignore everything I felt for her because of our careers? Because of what our boss had requested? Because of... *optics*?

That's how I knew I really fucked with her.

Being a part of the Nymphs coaching staff was a golden opportunity, my last real shot at making something of myself as far as professional basketball went. And I was still willing to risk it all for a chance with the woman who was arguably one of the best to ever do it at her position even if she didn't feel like it when she showed up to my room last night.

Now how we'd gone from her wanting to chat about that damn shot to me killin' her shit from the back, I wasn't exactly sure. But there wasn't a word of complaint in my vocabulary, a lazy grin on my lips as I watched her begin to stir from up under me so that she could groggily ask, "What time is it, Dre?"

Glancing back at the clock on the nightstand, I answered, "A little after three," not all that surprised when Selena popped up from the bed in a fury with a hissed, "*Shit.*"

Even if I wasn't as concerned with sticking to the "rules" placed on us, the last situation I imagined Selena wanted to be in was to have to make that long walk from my room to hers in front of her teammates, the frustration of the close call written all over her face as she rattled, "Why'd you let me sleep so long? Where's my phone? Where's my clothes?"

It took me a second to answer her questions since naked Selena with those fuckin' braids hanging down to her ass was a marvel. But eventually, I shook it off to reply, "Phones on the dresser, clothes are on the floor, and I let you sleep cause you were fuckin' tired, lil' baby."

For whatever reason, that stopped her in her tracks, a slick grin on her lips when she sarcastically groaned, "*Hmm.* I wonder why."

Standing up from the bed, I met her toe-to-toe, grabbing her ass in a low hug to say, "This dick. That's why," her lip immediately pulled between her teeth until I added, "Had you cuddled up on a nigga and everything."

Rolling her eyes, she pushed herself away from me to tease, "And now my side feels like I fell asleep on a pile of remotes."

With a chuckle, I went to grab a pair of shorts to throw on as I growled, "Fuck you, SeSa," only chuckling even more when she sang over her shoulder, *"You already did that, sir."* Then I waited until we were both mostly dressed to ask, "So you're good?"

Frowning, she fired back, "Why wouldn't I be good, Dre? We're both grown-ups, we smashed, and now it's time for us to get back to work."

Something about her word choice made my eyebrow pique when I asked, "Just like that, huh?"

Like I'd posed a stupid question, her eyes squinted as she cocked her head just slightly to respond, "Did you expect something else, *or…?*"

Considering all the thoughts I was having while I watched her sleep, it was safe to say I was definitely expecting something more - *a lot more.* Already ready to risk it all, ready to face the backlash head-on, ready to do whatever it took to make what was happening between us really go. But now that it was clear Selena had gotten all she wanted out of this, I felt silly for being so eager, shaking my head when I finally answered, "Nah. I'm just... happy to hear you feel the same way I do."

My response only made her smirk as she moved to stand back in front of me so that she could press her hands into my chest and challenge, "You're lying, aren't you, Dre?"

Instead of answering her question, I looked down at her and groaned, "Watch your mouth."

"Because you're gonna do what if I don't?" she pressed, a mischievous look in her eyes as she gnawed at the corner of her lip waiting for a response. And now that I knew exactly how she liked it, it was nothing for me to keep that same energy, slowly running a finger down the front of her neck as I replied, "You lucky I need you talkin' on the court tomorrow. Otherwise I'd bruise the fuck outta your throat."

"And that's supposed to make me wanna leave right now? Because... *shit*," she moaned with a shudder, making me chuckle as I muttered, "*Freaky ass...*"

"You're the one who said it!" she quickly defended, wrapping herself around me in a hug and pressing her chin into my chest to add, "But for the record, I'm into it. Very, very into it."

"Yeah, I bet you are," I groaned, meeting her lips for a quick peck that was a lot more *"in a relationship"* than *"post one-nighter"*.

Then again, if Selena wasn't overthinking things, there was no reason for me to either, doing my best to play along as she grinned up at me to say, "Thank you for the tips, Dre. All the tips. Game tips, life tips, and most importantly, di..."

Cutting her off with a laugh, I replied, "I got it,

Selena. Now get outta here before somebody wakes up early and sees you creeping around."

I expected the reminder to put the pep back into her step, but she didn't budge, studying my face intently before she challenged, "Not until you tell me the truth."

"The truth about what?"

"How last night… *this morning*… our time together really made you feel, because that *"feeling the same way I do"* you gave earlier was bullshit."

She was right.

Sure, I was following her lead so I wouldn't overstep any boundaries by trying to do too much too fast. But the truth was, I liked Selena. I liked her a lot, and I didn't feel as nonchalant about it as I was leading on.

Nah, I felt that shit deep, on a level I hadn't felt for anyone in a long ass time. But instead of fessing up right away and ruining this new dynamic before it could really play out, I came back at her with, "Just like nothing else was wrong with you last night, right?"

I expected the question to stumble her, but she only smirked. "How about you ask your dick that question since he's the one with the receipts?"

Like he knew what she was talking about, my shit got a little stiff in response, making her smirk also grow in size as I pulled her close enough to feel it when I asked, "You really wanna know how I feel, Ms. Samuels?" And after watching her short nod, I caught her eyes, holding her gaze for a moment past comfortable before I leaned in to whisper right against her lips, "Too bad."

"*Ugh*. Annoying. Goodbye," she rattled as she pushed away from me to head to the door, the whole thing amusing the hell out of me as I called after her, "Text me when you get in, aight?"

"*Like you can't just peek out and watch me walk down the hallway…*" she muttered, prompting me to explain, "If I do that, somebody might know where you're coming from."

"*Good point.* I'll text you," she agreed, pulling her hood back over her head to help the cause as I moved to open the door and let her out.

Not without one final tease though, a smirk on my lips as I suggested, "Might as well send some nudes while you're at it."

"You wish," she giggled on her way out, my back pressed against the door once I shut it behind her. Then I released a heavy sigh in an attempt to gather myself before I headed back to bed to wait for her text that took a little longer than I expected it to; though it was still enough to make me smile to myself in the dark on some weirdo shit once I read it and replied.

"Made it back to my room." - SeSa

"Good. Even though I wish you were still in mine." - Dre

"That's a dangerous game to play." - SeSa

Frowning like she could see me, I typed out a quick response.

"What? Wanting you here with me?" - Dre

"No. Wishing for something you know can't be." - SeSa

"Here we go with this shit," I groaned, annoyed with the fact that work authority was really ruling over my personal life too. Then again, maybe it wasn't just about Kat. Maybe Selena was leaning on that explanation when really, she just wasn't feelin' me the way I was feelin' her.

Instead of assuming anything, I asked her about it flat out.

"Because you don't want it to be?" - Dre

"Dre. Come on now. You know what it is." - SeSa

"Nah, you smashed and dashed on a nigga. I don't know shit." - Dre

I was really just teasing her since we both knew why she had to leave the way she did. But according to her response, she took offense anyway, using exaggerated punctuation to express what I knew would've been a passionate defense in person.

"Smashed and dashed?!? I stuck around to cuddle! That's gotta be worth somethin'!" - SeSa

"You only stayed to cuddle cause I wore that ass out." - Dre

"Okay, facts. But I'm also not mad about it, so…" - SeSa

"Get some rest, lil' baby. I'll see you later." - Dre

And I did see her later.

After what felt like only a catnap, I got up, showered, and met Selena along with the rest of the team down in the hotel lobby where we congregated before loading the charter bus that would take us to New York for our next game.

Once again, it was different than the men's league where this would've undoubtedly been a quick flight. But considering I didn't like to fly anyway, I wasn't complaining as I took a seat closer to the front of the bus, my subconscious already preparing for Selena to take the seat next to me and becoming a little disappointed when Sugar slid into it instead.

It was probably for the better.

I mean, the last thing we needed was to give people more reason to be suspicious about us. And by the deliberately neutral look on her face when she loaded the bus, it was clear Selena felt the same way; though she *did* give me a little wink on her way to the back that Sugar thankfully didn't notice since she was already too busy yapping about yesterday's game.

"I stayed up all night thinking about what we should've done differently, Dre. And you know what? Not a single damn thing came to mind. We played hard, we defended well, and we couldn't have put the ball in better hands for that last shot."

Nodding to agree, I replied, "Nine times outta ten, Selena is hittin' that. She just caught a bad angle at the rim."

It may not have been as obvious in live-action. But on film, it was clear as day, Sugar's enthusiasm only increasing when she asked, "So you saw that too?"

Considering the circumstances that led to me watching the play again - *and everything that happened afterwards* - it was hard not to grin as I answered, "Yeah, I did. And *I*… talked to her about it. She was a little bummed out."

"I can imagine," Sugar sighed before returning my grin to add, "But she's smiling today, so your pep talk must've worked."

"Yeah, I'd like to think so," I told her plainly, diverting my eyes to the window in hopes of not having to say anything more about it.

While it worked to some degree, I damn near

choked on my tongue when Sugar leaned in to whisper, "A little somethin' somethin' to go with those words might've done her one better, though."

Flinching with guilt, I let off the most awkward laugh as I groaned, "Come on, Sugar. We're talkin' about a player here."

"She's a woman first, Dre. And trust me when I tell you, this road can be a *very* lonely place."

It wasn't lost on me since I'd been there done that, once again nodding when I replied, "Yeah, I remember," even though Sugar was quick to disagree.

"Nah, it was different for you. I mean, I'm sure you encountered your fair share of women who followed teams city-to-city, knew the hotels certain teams stayed in and exactly where to "accidentally" show up. But for the women in this league, it's just not like that. You got to be lonely by choice where they don't always have one."

There was a lot of truth to her perspective, though I still couldn't help acknowledging, "Selena is a beautiful girl, Sugar. I can almost guarantee there's no shortage of men checkin' for her."

"Checkin' for her, sure. But on those quiet nights after a loss like yesterday, who's really there?" she asked, the question hitting on a personal level for *reasons*. And not only that, but now she had me wondering if Selena had really come to my room wanting to talk about the shot, or did she show up because she was just lonely.

Considering she had no idea about any of that, it was nothing for Sugar to move on with a sighed, "*Anyway*. New York has four of Geno Auriemma's former players, so we're in for a knockdown dragout kinda game tomorrow night. I'm thinking we'll…"

The rest of her words played in and out as I pulled out my phone to send Selena a text to make sure the way she left me was the same way she woke up this morning.

"You feelin' okay today, lil' baby?" - Dre

"Sleepy as hell, but yeah I'm good. You good?" - SeSa

"Better now that I know you're straight. Sugar was concerned to say the least." - Dre

"Concerned about what?" - SeSa

"Last night." - Dre

"She heard us???!" - SeSa

Chuckling, I gave a *"Mmhm"* to agree with whatever Sugar was talking about as I typed out my response.

"Not that, Selena. The game last night. The shot." - Dre

"Oh, that? I'm over it. Already onto NY." - SeSa

"Hmm. I wonder why…" - Dre

"That dick. That's why." - SeSa

"I'm going to sleep. See you in the next city, Jordan ;)" - SeSa

Now that I knew we were good - I mean, *she* was good - I gave Sugar my undivided attention, game-planning on how we'd guard New York's veteran center and making a note to practice it later during our walk-through. Then we started talking about basketball in general, Sugar's wealth of knowledge impressive as hell as I half-listened to her stories while checking my *Instagram* to discover Selena hadn't gone to sleep after all.

@SharpshooterSS liked @KageBeSteele's post

@SharpshooterSS left a comment on @Kage-BeSteele's post: Anytime, K ;)

"What is this all about?" I wondered, clicking over to the post that was a picture of Selena from yesterday's game; an action shot of her shooting a three-pointer with the caption, *"When her form is way better than yours… #Sharp-shooter #GimmeLessons"*

The photo was dope, but I found myself studying the caption even more; reading between the lines of both that and Selena's response to it. And once I put those two things with the picture she'd "liked" of the two of them after our first home game, I started to wonder if I wasn't the only one making sure Selena Samuels wasn't lonely; a thought I must've been wearing on my face since Sugar stopped whatever story she was in the middle of to ask, "Dre, are you listening to me?" before peeking over to my screen to see what had my attention.

After taking a look for herself, she gushed, "Oh, he's laying it on *real* thick, I see. This social media stuff makes gettin' at somebody way too easy. Back in my day, you had to see them in person, or know somebody who knew them, *or somethin'*. Now it's just a matter of finding their profile."

"Yeah, it's crazy," I agreed without giving too much, clicking out of the app before I gave the whole thing unnecessary energy. I mean, sure he'd posted about her multiple times and in response, she'd entertained it. But she was also the one who had come to me, the one who had woken up in my bed; *in my arms.*

As far as I was concerned, there was no competition.

And to make that clear, I logged back onto *Instagram* and "liked" the picture too.

She was ready.

I could tell by the hyper-focused expression on her face as she bobbed along to the pregame mix of songs playing throughout the arena long before any of the crowd arrived. It was just her, the music, and the basketball in her hand as she sat on the bench and dribbled the ball back and forth under her legs, totally zoned out in a way that looked all too familiar - *and was also attractive as hell.*

I'd seen plenty of pictures of Selena all dolled up; in magazines, on all the Nymphs promotional material, on *Instagram*. But there was something especially sexy about her game face in-person, easily taking its place as my second favorite - *only behind the face she made when she was riding me the other night* - as I continued to watch her dribble until I heard someone behind me say, "Well if it isn't DeAndre Leonard."

Turning around to see if the face matched the familiar voice, I couldn't help but smile once I saw that it did, my arms opening to receive the hug she already had extended as I replied, "Baby Bleu. What's up, girl? Long time, no see."

"I knowwww. How you been? Congrats on the new gig. That cardinal red looks just as good on you now as it did the first go-round," she teased with a pinch at my collared-Nymphs shirt that I'd paired with dark khakis and retro sneakers for tonight's game, going to a more casual look that Sugar had already clowned me about since she claimed I was *"serving Target worker realness"*.

Whatever that meant.

Shaking off the jokes from earlier, I replied, "I appreciate that, Bleu. And congrats to you too. I heard you're finally getting your own show."

Smiling with damn near all of her teeth, she gushed, *"Yesss.* It's still in the early development stages, but *Beyond the Bench with Bleu Taylor* is coming soon."

"That's what's up. You deserve it. Especially since you've been runnin' your mouth for as long as I've known you," I teased, catching a jab to the arm as she squealed, *"Oh, shut up!"* like she didn't know good and damn well how much her ass loved to talk.

It was how we met years ago at one of the Trojans media days, with her being an up-and-comer in the sports journalism world and me being a budding star in the league. Honestly, I'd only gone to talk to her cause she was fine as hell. But all it took was that first interview for me to know she was really about her shit, quickly establishing a respectful-working relationship between us. A relationship that only grew when she was hired to cover the team for what ended up being our championship season before moving onto bigger things out here in New York.

Just like back then, she was still her kindhearted, energetic self, a gentle hand against my arm as she said, "It's good to see you doing well, though. *Seriously.* And you know I can't wait to have you on the show."

"Let me do somethin' worth talkin' about first," I suggested, watching her lips twist in disbelief before she offered a rebuttal.

"Reviving your professional basketball career as a

coach for the Trojans sister team is definitely something worth talking about, Dre. But being able to talk about it from the perspective of a champion in both leagues would be even better."

"I'll see what I can do," was the most I could offer since it wasn't like I was the one out there on the court meaning I really didn't have *that* much control. But it seemed to be enough for Bleu who was being waved over by another media member that she gave the *"hold on"* finger to so she could respond to me.

Grabbing both of my hands, she expressed, "Either way, I'm proud of you. And I look forward to witnessing more of your success which better include a televised-win tonight so I can get a happy postgame interview from Selena Samuels."

Again, the most I could offer was, "I'll see what I can do," a slight grin on Bleu's face as she gave my hands a squeeze before moving along. And I felt just as proud watching her call the shots with her camera team which was a huge step-up from the tiny recorder she used to carry around us back in the day, something I thought about making a move to comment on until I felt a basketball hit my shin.

"*Ooh.* Sorry," Selena said in reference to the ball she must've bounced off her foot during her pregame daze, getting ready to pop up from her seat to come grab it until I stopped her with my hand and picked it up myself.

"Don't be," I told her as I tossed it back, taking the seat next to her to ask, "You ready to go?"

"*Always,*" she replied shortly, already back to her mindless dribbling as I agreed, "I can tell. I see it in your eyes tonight."

It was supposed to be a compliment, but it didn't seem like Selena received it that way, a scowl on her face as she muttered more to herself than me, "Surprised you even noticed."

"What's that supposed to mean?" I asked with squinted eyes, her attitude catching me off-guard. But instead of responding to me, she stopped her dribbling to look past me, my attention going in the same direction once she stood up to greet the last person I expected to see.

Or rather, the last person *we* expected to see according to Selena's surprised reaction when she asked, "*Kage*? What are you doing here?"

"Had some press shit in the city earlier, so I thought I'd swing by and check you out," he answered with a shrug as he moved to pull her in for a hug and a cheek kiss that didn't seem to make Selena uncomfortable.

In fact, she seemed so cool with it that I caught a little attitude myself by the time Kage greeted me with a casual, "What's good, fam?" replying with a head nod and a nonchalant, "*Sup,*" before sitting back to watch the two interact.

I would've been lying if I didn't admit how jealous I felt seeing Kage "lay it on thick" as Sugar had called it, running a hand down his crisp white tee as he told her, "I ain't got my jersey on today, but you know who I'm here for, right?"

Smirking, Selena replied, "Your support is much appreciated, Kage; *by all of us,*" brushing a hand against his arm to add, "I need to go finish my pregame routine."

"You do that, baby," he groaned as he watched her move back to the court, the whole thing annoying the fuck outta me since Selena hadn't bothered to correct him about that *"baby"* shit. And I suppose that made him comfortable enough to take the seat next to mine as we both watched her run through drills, my scowl really taking shape when he commented, "That's a special breed of woman right there. Not many like her. I mean, she's fine as hell *and* a baller? Got her own money, a degree, *and* MVP potential? Yeah, I'ma have to wife that."

Before I could bite my tongue, I blurted, "I think she's good, bruh," the possessive energy surprising me since it wasn't like Selena was really mine to claim.

I mean, sure we'd had a night; a damn good one at that. But it wasn't like she'd made a big deal about it - *or about us* - making me feel uncertain as hell when Kage turned my way to ask, "You mean that? Or you just blockin' cause you want her for yourself?"

It was a complicated question. But coming from him in this particular moment, it was just flat-out annoying, my eyes tight when I growled, "I ain't gotta block shit."

Instead of taking the hint to back off, he only chuckled, standing up and pushing a breath out of his nose as he replied, "*Hmph.* Heard you, my nigga." Then he gave me a pat to the shoulder to say, "Good luck with that, champ," before moving to take pictures with some of the other courtside fans who were now showing up, leaving me in a bad mood that I had to shake off so I could do my job. But even when the game started, the situation still sat heavy on my mind, making me wonder if now was the time to act on my feelings for Selena before Kage could really fuck shit up.

NINE

A TWO-GAME ROAD trip had complicated *everything*.

Learning more about Dre during our flight was one thing. Going to him for advice after the game was another. But fucking the man, cuddling afterwards, and then feeling a way over seeing him chat with another woman to the point that I let *Kage* get more play than usual?

Yeah, shit was *real* complicated. And unfortunately, nothing in my world was slowing down anytime soon, forcing me to try and think on the fly which was why I called myself bringing it up to Ari as she taped my ankle for tonight's home game in a few hours.

With a smirk on her face, she said, "I gotta be honest, Selena. I'm kinda jealous right now."

Rolling my eyes, I groaned, "*Ugh*. Don't be. Nothing about this is envy-worthy."

Instead of agreeing, she looked up at me to give a reminder I really didn't need since, *well*, my body remembered every damn thing. And because it remembered everything, I literally shivered when she said, "Sis, you got dicked down by DeAndre Leonard on the late-night tip, and you have Kage Steele waiting in the wings. A little bit older and a little bit younger. A seasoned veteran and an eager rookie. A firmly molded man and a moldable one. The best of both worlds."

"Sounds all fine and dandy; doesn't feel that way at all," I sighed, pulling the top half of my braids back into a ponytail as Ari tapped my shin to signal she was done.

Well, done with the taping that was supposed to help the tenderness I felt after the game against New York. Not done with the interrogation, a confused look on her face when she asked, "So what's the problem?"

Again, I sighed, propping my leg up so that I could put my shoe back on as I answered, "I don't really want Kage. And I can't have Dre."

"Why not? And don't say Kat, cause that shit with them has always been a figment of your imagination."

"I wouldn't say all that. But I *can* admit I made some assumptions about their involvement," I told her, catching a mean side eye and changing my response because of it. "Okay, maybe a lot of assumptions."

"Girl, you created a whole relationship and added your name to their wedding invitation list," she replied with a laugh that I did my best to ignore as I fixed my shoelaces and groaned, "*Anyway*. Even if he's not with Kat, I still respect her wanting us to keep things professional. And after seeing him be all buddy-buddy with Bleu…"

Before I could finish, Ari cut me off. "Selena, you do realize you neutralized that shit by flirting with Kage right in that man's face, right?"

"We didn't flirt. I was just a little nicer than usual," I defended, catching another side eye that had me avoiding eye contact altogether since it made me feel guilty as hell.

Still, that didn't mean Ari wasn't going to make her point, using extra emphasis to say, "*Intentionally* a little nicer, as a response to seeing Dre conversing with Bleu. Which, *by the way*, I'm pretty sure she's friendly like that with everybody."

Considering I had experienced it firsthand during my postgame interview, I would've been lying if I didn't agree with Ari's claims, shaking my head as I replied, "I know, I know. I was trippin'. It just rubbed me the wrong way. I mean, I could feel him watching me, and then she came along, *and...*"

"You were jealous, so you tried to make him jealous," she finished for me, watching me nod as she continued, "I get it, Selena. But also, be a grown-up. Stop fuckin' around and just tell that fine ass man how you feel after he dropped that dick off in you somethin' proper."

If my feelings were only sex-related, they would've been a lot easier to speak on. But the truth was, it was deeper than that. The connection I felt with Dre was beyond just the physical. I mean, he knew shit about me that not even Ari knew and that was saying a lot since I was an *extremely* private person when it came to my personal business. But with Dre, it was just... *easy*, natural, comfortable to the point that I really hadn't thought twice about being so open. And it certainly helped that he reciprocated that same energy, only making me want to share more of myself so that I could learn more about him in the process.

Still, what was simple in those moments wasn't so simple big picture, a somber expression on my face when I finally told Ari, "First of all, it's not just about the dick. And second of all, tell him how I feel for what? It's not like we can really do shit about it right now anyway."

Between the busyness of the season and Kat's concern about the optics, anything more than what we'd already done was a major stretch. Though Ari didn't quite see it that way when she suggested, "Again, be a grown-up. There's *plenty* of things you can do about it, Selena. Just don't do it in this facility until y'all are serious enough to take on the inevitable, i.e. people in your business."

Because it was sound advice - *and because I needed to get to the court* - I grabbed my phone and hopped down from the training table to tell her, "Thanks, Ari," absorbing all the good energy from the hand she pressed against my arm when she replied, "Anytime, babe. And let me know how that ankle feels after the game. I'll write you up a recovery plan just in case."

Giving her a nod, I headed out of the training room, mindlessly scrolling through my phone as I traveled down the hall towards the court's entryway. But when I turned the corner, I walked right up on a conversation clearly not meant for me to hear, my eyebrow piqued as I slipped behind the wall to listen in as one of the Trojans support staff said, "Mannnn, I can't believe the Lloyds really got you coaching in that boring ass league. I know good and damn well you'd rather be with us."

"Boring ass league?" I whispered to myself with a frown that only grew tighter when, instead of correcting the man, Dre replied, "An opportunity is an opportunity, G. It's honest work."

"Yeah, honestly trash as fuck. I mean, I don't know

how you don't fall asleep on the bench every game. *Wait.* Yes, I do. Some of them bitches be fine as hell," he commented with this annoying ass laugh that had me hot as I hissed, *"Bitches?"* while Dre passively suggested, "Relax, man."

Of course the man didn't relax, really going in when he insisted, "Can't call themselves the Nashville Nymphos and not expect a nigga to see 'em that way; especially with a head coach named Sugar. Yeah, I'll take some sugar alright…"

Again, Dre was passive as hell when he corrected, "It's the Nymphs, G. Not the Nymphos."

"Nymphs. Nymphos. Same difference. All I know is, maybe if they played in some lingerie or somethin', a nigga like me would actually fuck wit' it. But until then, they can keep taking their boring asses overseas to play for the mothafuckas who don't know any better."

That was the final straw as I peeled around the corner with my finger pointed in his direction and growled, "You got a lot of fuckin' nerve," his eyes wide in shock as Dre stepped in front of me to try and stop me.

Keyword: Try

Pushing past him, I snapped, "Nah, this mothafucka thinks shit is sweet like his ass doesn't clean-up after grown men for a living. All-time discarded towel catcher, and got the nerve to talk shit about us? You do realize you're nothin' but a glorified ballboy, right? A grown ass man rushing to pick-up sweaty booty warm-up pants and hand out water bottles. How pathetic."

"Selena, relax," Dre urged with a lot more aggression than he was giving ol' boy earlier, only making me angrier as I told him, "Nah, fuck that. Y'all can both kiss my ass."

The man took that as a cue to dismiss himself while he had the chance. But Dre didn't have it so easy since he was the one who still had to deal with me after the fact, his head cocked when he asked, "What I do?"

Pointing in the direction of the perpetrator, I answered, "Lettin' that mothafucka run his mouth about our league with no repercussions, that's what. If you wanna be with the Trojans so bad, why don't you just leave, Dre? We were good before you, and we'll be good after you."

Once the words left my lips, I realized how harsh they sounded. But I wasn't taking them back, not even after seeing the somehow attractively-somber look on Dre's face when he took a step closer to me and asked, "That's how you feel?"

The intensity in his stare made my heart race, but I wasn't backing down from this, crossing my arms over my chest to respond, "Yes, that's how I feel. I mean, you really think we play overseas because the people don't know any better?"

His groaned, *"I didn't say that"* got drowned out by the rest of my spiel when I ranted, "You got to go play overseas as a choice, to try and hide from the pile of bullshit you left over here in the states. But for me? It's not an option. It's how I take care of those I love; how we all take care of those we love because this league alone doesn't allow us to do that."

"I know that, Selena," he sighed, almost annoyedly like it wasn't partially his fault that I had to explain the shit in the first place.

Because of that fact, I had no problem exclaiming, "Then act like it!"

Dre's eyes immediately tightened as he pressed his body against mine with what was essentially a push with no hands since I was forced to step back, his glare dangerously dark when he looked down at me to say, "Nah, see. What you're not gonna do is raise your fuckin' voice at me about this shit."

My head told me to stand down. *But my ego?* Sis was alive and well even while being lodged between Dre and the wall behind me, my chest heaving when I snapped, "Maybe if you would've kept this same energy with him, I wouldn't have to."

Just as Dre opened his mouth to respond, one of the arena's security guards strolled past, doing his best to act like he wasn't in our business when he gave Dre a nod and me a no-lip smile on his way out to the court. But the brief interruption was enough to change Dre's demeanor as he took a tiny step back to ask, "*Look.* Can we just talk about this later?"

"Nah, I have nothin' else to say," I replied, using the bit of space he'd created between us to make a move towards the court even as Dre followed me and groaned, *"Selena, come on."*

"I have a game to prepare for, Coach Leonard. I suggest you do the same. Well, that's *if* you still care to stick around us boring basketball bitches," I snarled with a roll of my eyes that had Dre snatching me back by my wrist.

Well, maybe it wasn't a snatch; more of a gentle grab. But in this moment, everything felt intensified, his, *"Don't do that"* clashing with my, *"Don't touch me"* as I yanked away and continued my pursuit towards the rack of basketballs so that I could begin my pregame routine. And I suppose because he knew how important this part was for my psyche, he left me alone which was honestly his best bet - *and our opponent's worst nightmare.*

With my adrenaline still pumping from my argument with Dre, and a little bit of *"remind these mothafuckas what you're made of"* coursing through my veins after dealing with that lame ass ballboy, I played a game worth memorializing, putting up numbers unseen as far as the Nymphs organization went.

Forty-nine points which was just four shy of tying the overall league record.

A perfect seven-for-seven from behind the arc.

Twelve rebounds and ten assists to round out my triple-double.

And most importantly, a win that just so happened to be over my former team.

Before the game, I'd tried not to put so much emphasis on that part since it wasn't like this was my first time playing against them since forcing my trade out of LA. But it definitely made the victory a little sweeter to celebrate with my Nymphs teammates and coaches.

Well, except for Dre who must've thought he'd bury the hatchet when he acknowledged, "Good shit tonight, SeSa."

"Selena is fine," I corrected, blowing past him to go sign autographs and take pictures with the fans. But even then, I could still feel him watching me from afar, an amused smirk on his face that somehow told me this wasn't the end of our run.

TEN

I WAS DONE with the bullshit.

I'd given her space, I'd given her time to process, and I'd even sent her a text to apologize. But now, this little one-sided beef had gone on for far too long. And to be real, I missed my friend.

So that's how I found myself sitting in Selena's locker spot hours before our game later tonight, knowing she'd be arriving earlier than her teammates since it was a part of her routine to get in some extra work before everyone else showed up. And like clock-work, she strolled in with a new look I wasn't expecting, her long braids replaced with a curly ponytail sitting at the top of her head and her usual sweatpants and sneakers exchanged for a pair of skin-tight jeans and strappy-sandal heels that had her legs looking especially long - *had her looking especially sexy.*

She knew it too. I could tell by the smirk on her lips when she caught me ogling and asked, "Can I help you with somethin', Coach Leonard?"

Standing up from my seat so she could replace it

with her duffle bag, I answered, "Yeah, actually you can."

Without giving me eye contact, she followed, "Is it basketball-related?"

"Yeah, it is," I told her, knowing that was only partially true since there was a lot more than just basketball we needed to discuss.

But considering that was my only way in, I rolled with it, watching her begin to unpack her bag as she tossed over her shoulder, "So… what's up?"

Releasing a heavy sigh, I took a moment to choose my words carefully, wishing I had her eyes when I shared, "Selena, you know I respect what y'all do on the court more than the average person. I wouldn't be here if I didn't."

"You sure about that? Or are you only here cause this was your "opportunity"?" she asked with an obvious lick of sarcasm even though I couldn't see her face.

Still, that didn't deter me from being honest when I replied, "That's what got me here, yeah. But that's not what keeps me showing up every day. It's you - *y'all*. Seeing how hard y'all work, how bad y'all want it, how committed y'all are to bringing the championship to Nashville. I respect y'all as ball players, and I would never allow myself to be associated with somethin' I didn't truly believe in."

It was my truth regardless of how she received it. But I was happy when she, at least, turned around to respond, "Look, Dre. I don't need you to prove that to me. I'm gonna go hard regardless of what you think, and my game speaks for itself. *But as for these other eleven women rockin' a Nymphs jersey?* They deserve to have you sticking up for them in their absence. They deserve to have their sacrifices recognized and respected. They deserve *better*."

With a nod, I agreed, "You're right, which is why I texted you an apology."

That made her pull her eyes away, back to getting her personal items organized in her locker as she admitted, "Honestly, I didn't even read it. I saw your name pop up and immediately deleted it."

"*Damn*. That's rude as hell," I halfway laughed, not all that surprised since I knew just how bullheaded she could be. But really, it was part of what I liked about her, her passion towards whatever she believed in even if it was against me.

As expected, she didn't feel bad about it either, rattling off an unapologetic, "Sorry not sorry. You had me fucked up."

I was quick to correct, "No, *he* had you fucked up. I just didn't do my part as an ally. So for that, *and because you deleted it when I said it the first time*, I'm sorry."

Again, she turned back my way, this time with a smile that lowkey made my heart flutter when she replied, "I appreciate that."

"Though I must say, lighting a fire under your ass got you the lead story on *Sportscenter, so…*" I trailed teasingly, catching the meanest side eye as she damn near growled, "Don't try me, Dre."

With a shrug, I purposely gassed the situation, plopping down in Talia's empty spot next to hers to add, "I'm just sayin'. Maybe ol' boy had a point about you boring basketball bi…"

Before I could even get the last word out - *I wasn't going to get the last word out* - Selena jabbed a finger towards the exit and snapped, "Get out," only making me laugh for real as I stood back up to tell her, "Nah, seriously though. I *uh…* I was wondering if maybe we could make some plans for after the game. Catch up on lost time thanks to that cold ass shoulder you've been given me as of late."

Because we'd only taken a step back from our night spent together in Connecticut, we really had more than just lost time to catch up on. And I was glad to see Selena caught my vibe, a smirk on her lips when she slickly replied, "That can possibly be arranged."

"What, you gotta run it past your little boyfriend first or somethin'?" I asked teasingly, watching as her lips immediately twisted into a frown.

"My little boyfriend? I just *know* you aren't talking about Kage?"

"How'd you know I was talkin' about Kage then?" I pressed, wishing I'd snapped a picture of the shocked expression on her face once she realized she'd gotten caught up in her own words.

She did her best to recover though, groaning an exaggerated, "*Anyway.* Kage is just a huge Nymphs supporter."

"*More like a huge Selena Samuels supporter,*" I muttered as she shot another side eye my way, this time with a smile that had me quick to add, "But really, it ain't none of my business no way. I just wanna spend some time with my friend."

"Oh, so we're friends again?" she asked, her eyebrow piqued like it was really all that surprising.

Then again, considering she was the one who was mad in the first place, maybe it really was news which was why I replied, "Ask yourself that question, lil' baby."

Averting her eyes, she put a finger to her chin to

literally do it, using some extra fluffy voice to ask, "Do you wanna be Jordan's friend, Selena?" and then changing it up to respond, "Hmm... I don't know let me think about it."

"You play too much," I told her with a laugh, shaking my head as she caught my hand with a serious look in her eyes.

A look that had me a little concerned until she finally blurted, "Dre, I'm sorry too. For... blowing up on you like that the other day. It wasn't *totally* your fault that that guy was being an ass. It's just we catch shit like that *all* the time, for no reason other than people seeing us as an easy target for disrespect. Trolls on the internet telling us to get back in the kitchen, talking about our style of play, talking about what we should and shouldn't do like they'd care about our game either way. I guess I'm *just...* sick of it."

Nodding, I gave her hand a squeeze. "I get it, lil' baby. No explanation needed." And she seemed to be pleased with that, licking her lips before bringing back up our other order of business.

"So these plans you speak of..."

"We'll talk after the game. Right now, I need you focused," I insisted, earning myself an annoyed grunt as she turned back towards her locker to complain.

"Shouldn't have come in here lookin' all good and smellin' even better if you really expected me to stay focused on the game, Dre."

"Shit, I had to come correct since you ain't been wantin' to talk to ya boy lately," I reminded her, surely sounding pitiful as hell even though it was the truth.

A truth that Selena took full advantage of when she sang, "Aww, you missed me?"

"Yeah. Actually, I did," I admitted, pulling her into a hug that she only halfway resisted. And when I started kissing on her neck, that halfway turned into not at all, a moan slipping from the back of her throat that only made me go harder since I really did miss her.

Well, missed being like *this* with her, that one night together not being nearly enough as I grabbed a handful of her ass to pull her closer while she groaned, "You better stop before somebody comes in here and sees us."

"Just give me a lil' somethin' to hold me over until tonight," I pleaded, nibbling at her ear before I whispered, "I've been starved."

That really made her crumble, her hands wrapped around the back of my head to keep me close as I licked and kissed her skin until she gulped in response to Mikayla walking in singing, "Anything for Selenaaaaoh my God."

"*Shit,*" Selena hissed, extracting herself from my hold as I did my best to cover with an overacted, "Mikayla. *Hey.* You're here early."

What she'd seen was written all over her face when she grinned and replied, "Looks to me like I'm right on time, Coach Leonard," moving to drop her bag off in her locker as she added, "Trying to take after my dear teammate here by showing up early to get a little extra work in, and now I know the real secret to her success. Not mad about it. Not mad about it at all."

Ignoring Mikayla completely, Selena blurted, "*I...* need to go change," taking off towards the more private dressing area to do so as I scrubbed a hand down my facial hair and tried to figure out how to best handle the situation. But considering how much Mikayla had witnessed, I quickly realized I didn't have many options other than the truth.

So that's what I went with, moving closer to her locker to request, "Mikayla, if you could not say anything about what you just walked in on, I'd greatly appreciate it."

With her, I knew keeping quiet would be a stretch since the girl not only loved to talk about anything under the sun, but she loved to do that shit publicly. And I could only hope there was some weight to her, "That ain't no problem." Though I shouldn't have been surprised when she waited until I was already walking away to add, "Just make sure I get an invite to the wedding!"

Shaking my head, I continued out of the locker room, getting ready to head towards the court until I heard someone behind me yell, "Dre!" And after peeking back to see the source of the voice, I caught Kat doing a lightweight jog in her heels to get to where I was standing before she pulled her phone out to breathlessly say, "*Look*. Don't be mad. And I'm doing my best to get it scrubbed from the internet as soon as possible. *But…* you should probably see this."

My face automatically scrunched in confusion since it wasn't like I was super active as far as social media went. The occasional post to let strangers know I was still alive, but nothing out of the ordinary which made it even more shocking when Kat handed me her phone to show what had just recently been posted on *Instagram* by one of the popular gossip blog pages, *Spilling That Hot Tea*.

It was a picture of me, but also not exactly a picture of me; my mugshot from years ago printed onto a t-shirt worn by the Trojans rookie who had apparently shared it to his *Instagram* story last night with the caption, *"New Nymphs merch. #FreeDreLeonard"*

His caption was one thing, and *STHT*'s was another, theirs bringing even more life to the situation.

"#PostAndDelete Looks like @KageBeSteele feels a way about former Tennessee Trojans player @DreLeonard being back in Nashville. Or maybe there's more to the story? Stay tuned cause you know we're gonna get the tea..."

"Wow. This little mothafucka is bold as hell," I groaned, growing angrier by the second as Kat snatched her phone back and agreed with me.

"He's an asshole is what he is. I mean, what would even make him do this?"

Thinking back to our short conversation in New York, I could only sigh as I told her, "I know exactly why he did it," before asking, "He's not coming to the game today, is he?"

I was already planning to have more than just a few words with him when Kat shook her head to answer, "I don't think so."

"Wise choice," I thought as I told her, *"Good.* Let's keep it that way for the rest of the season."

It seemed like a no-brainer to me since it was obvious his ass was up to no good. But Kat wasn't quite onboard, her expression torn when she replied, "I... don't know if I can do that, Dre. I mean, maybe we can suspend him for a couple games as like a warning. But having him courtside has boosted our social media engagement massively."

"So his ass just gets to do whatever he wants, play with my reputation, and I just gotta deal with it?" I snapped, damn near seething when Kat had the nerve to respond from a business mind instead of a personal one.

"Play defense, Dre. Get ahead of his ass. Go comment that it was just an inside joke, or that you're launching an exclusive clothing line. Don't let him win."

Shaking my head, I was quick to disapprove. "Nah, I don't do that internet shit. I'll just pull up on his bitch ass."

"And get an updated mugshot for him to make another shirt out of?! No, Dre. That's not how we roll around here. I need you to be smarter than that. If not for me, at least for my father, for Sugar, for the team, for Selena."

She was trying to use Selena as a motivator when really this all started with her. But since Kat didn't know all of the details of that - *and I wasn't interested in giving them* - I did my best to calm down enough for her to believe me when I said, "Yeah, aight Kat. Thanks for the heads-up."

The game was over and won, and I still had an attitude.

It was like no matter how hard I tried to shake Kage's little *Instagram* stunt, it kept coming back to me in different ways; wondering how many people had seen it now that it was really making its rounds on the internet even after he'd deleted it from his page, wondering where he'd even gotten that stupid ass idea from, wondering why he was so pressed to try and make a mockery of that time in my life like I hadn't already lived through the shit while being in the public eye.

Actually, I knew the answer to that one. He wanted Selena and for whatever reason saw me as a threat, surely thinking his post would be some sort of deterrent. But unfortunately for him, Selena already knew the truth. In fact, she knew more than the average person, having a much better understanding of everything surrounding that dark period and fuckin' with me even harder after the fact.

So really, he just looked dumb. At least, that's what I kept trying to tell myself as I sat through Sugar's postgame speech that included an announcement about us having the day off tomorrow. An announcement that had the room going up in celebration as Selena peeked over and shot me a wink that I responded to with what must've been a strained smile since Selena was quick to respond with a look of confusion.

Because she had other postgame obligations, she couldn't address it until after those were taken care of, walking straight over to me when she was finished with her press conference to ask, "Hey. You okay?"

"Yeah, I'm good. We still on for tonight?" I questioned, thinking that would not only help take my mind off the Kage situation but also keep her from pressing me about my demeanor from earlier too.

Smirking, she challenged, "You mean, still on for the plans you've yet to tell me about?"

"Had to make sure we won first. Cause you know that shit would've changed your whole attitude if we hadn't," I insisted, watching as she knowingly nodded to agree.

"This is true. But considering we *did* win, what was that face about earlier?"

"So she really did notice," I thought, doing my best to play it down when I answered, "It's nothin' worth giving energy towards."

"But still somethin', so just tell me," she pressed, her doe eyes sitting even wider than usual as she waited on an explanation. And since it was clear she wasn't going to let it go, I released another sigh before giving a sample of the truth.

"Your little boyfriend called himself making jokes on the internet last night."

With a chuckle, she was quick to scold, "First of all, quit with that little boyfriend shit. Second of all, what kinda jokes? Jokes about you? Why would he be making jokes about you?"

Scrubbing a hand against the back of my head, I answered, "We might've had a conversation. Back in New York."

"*Back in New York?*" she repeated with a frown that only grew tighter once I told her, "Yeah. About you."

"*Oh God…*" she groaned with a roll of her eyes, her frown turning into more of a disappointed scowl when she asked, "Dre, why would you even entertain that nonsense?"

"Ask yourself that question, Selena. I mean, if it wasn't for you entertaining him first, I wouldn't have had to."

"And if it wasn't for you and Bleu, I wouldn't have…"

"*Wait.* Me and Bleu? Aint' shit goin' on with me and Bleu. That's just my homegirl."

"And I'm supposed to know that how?" she fired back with her eyes tight and her arms crossed defensively, the sight making me chuckle once I realized - *we're really arguing about this shit?*

Gently pulling her arms apart, I answered, "How about you try asking instead of assuming? Ain't like I've ever hid anything from you, so why would I start now?"

Because she knew I was right, she only responded with a sigh, slightly changing the subject when she asked, "So what did Kage say about you?"

Instead of giving a verbal explanation, I just pulled it up on my phone and handed it to her so she could see it for herself, watching her eyes frantically scan the screen as she rambled, "This is stupid. He's an idiot. Don't let him get to you, Dre."

"Easier said than done, Selena. I've been workin' real hard to rebuild my reputation in this city. So anybody who tries to fuck with that is a problem," I told her, still not exactly sure of how I wanted to handle it but very clear on the fact that it had to be done.

To my surprise, Selena agreed, handing my phone back and pulling out her own as she replied, "I'm pretty sure I can find out where he lives. We can go over there and handle this right now."

"Was... *not* expecting you to see it my way," I admitted with a little chuckle, her whole ride-or-die vibe amusing the hell out of me and lowkey turning me on all at once.

That feeling only grew when I watched her aggressively type something on her phone while replying, "People tryna clown others on the internet for clout or whatever is corny as fuck. And to be real, I thought he was better than that."

Even if I didn't know all the ins and outs of their involvement, I had a feeling she wasn't lying about thinking better of him since I was sure she wouldn't have allowed herself to be associated with him at all otherwise. And honestly, after watching lil' homie ball this past season, I kind of thought better of him too. But when it came down to it, I knew it wasn't all that uncommon for niggas to get outta pocket when there was a woman involved, which was why it felt a little easier to swallow once I wrapped Selena in a hug and teased, "See what you make people do, lil' baby. Got us all acting outta character."

Because there was no one else around, she sank into my hold, her hands pressed into my chest when she looked up at me and asked, "Was that post *really* about me, though? Or was he just comin' for the old man?"

"You gonna get enough of callin' me old like I ain't still got it," I warned, watching her nose scrunch as she snapped her head back and repeated my claims.

"*Still got it?* Uh… I would like to see it."

"Check my credentials. That banner hanging up in the arena didn't get there by itself," I reminded her without even realizing I was setting myself up.

Selena knew exactly what she was doing though, a mischievous look in her eyes when she taunted, "Yeah, that's from the bounce you had *years* ago. I'm talkin' about right now. *Today*. Can you still throw it down like you used to, or nah? Cause your mind is probably saying yes, but I can hear your knees screaming nah."

On one hand, I knew I shouldn't have been letting her talk me into anything. But on the other hand, I was curious myself, knowing it had been a while since the last time I even tried to do what she was egging on. And once that got into my head, I couldn't let it go, giving a little shrug as I told her, "Guess it's only one way to find out."

Of course she was satisfied with that, grinning as she led the way out onto the court I used to call home as a player, seeing it in that light hitting differently than the times I'd walk out as a part of the Nymphs coaching staff this season. And once Selena grabbed a ball for me to use and tossed it my way, I swear I could hear murmurs from the crowd cheering in my ear, sending me into a zone as I took a few dribbles towards the rim and rose up for a dunk that felt… *amazing*.

Invigorating.

Felt… "*Booooring*! Come on, Dre! Talia could've done that!"

Smirking her way, I dribbled the ball back towards the top of the key, thinking of another dunk to show off and deciding on a simple three-sixty that Selena reacted to with a golf clap.

"Okay, okay. I'd give that like a seven point five in the dunk contest. Now show me somethin' worth a ten."

Laughing her off, I dropped the ball to my feet so that I could remove my dress shirt for more flexibility, taking my time to unbutton it since the first two dunks had me a little winded. And once I got it off, I realized Selena had been ogling me with glossy eyes the entire time, tossing the shirt her way to snap her out of her lusty daze as I told her, "You really tryna have a nigga out here hurt. I mean, no warm-up or nothin' and you expect a dunk worth a ten?"

"Come on. I'll throw you an alley-oop," she insisted,

dropping both her duffle bag and my shirt then sticking her hands out for me to toss her the ball. And because it was in good fun, I followed through, Selena throwing up a perfectly-timed dime for me to dunk with ease.

"*Ugh.* I wish I could dunk. I'd be so good at it," she whined as she grabbed the rebound, making me chuckle when I teased, "How you figure? I mean, you ain't even all that good at laying it up, *so…*"

"Oh wowwww. Is that a challenge? Cause these heels *do* come off," she threatened, only making me laugh harder as I moved her way to snatch the ball out of her hands.

Well, *tried* to snatch the ball out of her hands, Selena turning away to guard it when she pressed, "You're scared I'm gonna whoop that ass, huh?"

Shaking my head, I groaned, "Selena, stop. I don't want you gettin' hurt. Not on my watch."

Considering the scope that was already on us for our personal shit, I could only imagine how Kat would react if I did something to *really* jeopardize the season. But leave it to Selena's competitive ass to already be unstrapping her heels as she said, "First to five, counting by ones and twos. Make it, take it."

Because I knew she wouldn't let it go - *and that I could make it to five real quick* - I agreed, "Yeah, aight. Let's go then." And that was all Selena needed to hear as she kicked her shoes out of the way and checked the ball up, taking a few dribbles to her left and putting up a quick shot that went in all net.

"Jordan DeAndre Leonard, you are guarding the leading three-point shooter in the league right now. You better put some respect on that shit and step up," she gloated, amusing the hell out of me as I bounced the ball her way to check up again. And this time when she took her little dribbles to create some space, I stole the ball from her, setting up for a three-pointer that was easy to get off thanks to our height difference.

Once the ball went through the net, I did a little bragging of my own, catching the smirk on her lips when I announced, "Tied up, lil' baby. Now put some respect on *that* shit," pointing to the championship banner hanging in the rafters.

With a confident nod, she bounced the ball my way and said, "I'm gonna have my own to point at one day. Just watch."

There was no doubt in my mind that that time was coming sooner than later. But right now, I was only focused on our game of one-on-one, backing her down to the rim as I replied, "Nah, *you* just watch."

She was giving me a lot of body, but it still wasn't enough to keep me from scoring on a hook shot right over her head that somehow made her fall in the process. And while she probably expected me to apologize for it, I didn't, looking down at her to snarl, "*What?* I'm supposed to feel sorry for you? Get your ass up and play ball, SeSa."

From the determined look on her face, I could tell I'd awoken the beast, not all that surprised when she checked the ball and immediately got right in my face to play real defense. And even though I was still able to get a shot off, I missed it, Selena rushing to chase down the rebound in her jeans and setting up for another jump-shot I was too slow to defend.

"Tied up. *Again*," she sang as I grabbed the ball from under the rim, shaking my head as I bounced it to her to check and found myself really d'ing up too since there was no way I could let her beat me. But that didn't mean she wasn't going to try, taking a few aggressive dribbles towards the hoop and then crossing backwards for a stepback jumpshot that made me stumble as she fired it to the rim and I… *shit, my ankle.*

By the time the ball went through the hoop, I was already on the ground, Selena holding a hand over her mouth like she couldn't believe what she'd done before rushing over to check on me. But once she got close enough, I pulled her down on top of me, playfully wrestling her into a hug as she whined, "You only faked an injury cause you knew I was about to win!"

"Nah, my shit really is a little tweaked," I admitted, burying my face in her neck to add, "But yeah, that's the story you can tell yourself."

Between my response and my facial hair tickling her skin, she was all giggles when she announced, "Bucket List item number 368 - Break Dre Leonard's ankles. *Check.*"

"Wowww, really?" I groaned with a chuckle, tickling her into a fit of giggles as she joked, "And you were worried about Kage messin' with your reputation. You're lucky nobody saw *that* shit."

"I'll give 'em somethin' to see alright," I mocked, nibbling at her neck in a way that had her quick to moan, "*Mmm.* Your place or mine?"

"It's up to you," I told her, knowing the location didn't even matter.

She was getting this dick regardless.

Pressing her hands onto my chest, she created enough space between us to look me in the eyes and say, "Come to mine. And bring a bag just in case."

"That's what you want?"

"I mean, we do have a day off, *so...*" she trailed, gnawing at the corner of her lip like she was already making plans for more than just tonight. And considering how much catching up we had to do, I was down for whatever, quick to express that with a simple request.

"Text me your address."

ELEVEN

I RARELY INVITED people into my space.

There was something especially solitudinous about it; a word I'd only learned so that I could properly describe the townhouse I'd purchased on my own two years ago when I moved back to Nashville after having a roommate during my time spent in Los Angeles.

Back then, living with someone made the most sense since, *well*, the city was expensive as hell on a rookie salary and having my own spot was wasteful as hell when I spent most of the year playing overseas anyway. But I missed all the perks that came with living alone and moving to the Green Hills area was a no-brainer since not only was it nice but the people tended to mind their own business.

It was also a great change of speed when compared to the East Nashville neighborhood I'd grown up in; the same neighborhood my father still lived in even after I'd offered to put him and his family in something nicer.

"You already paid it off, Selena. No reason for me to move just so these hippies can buy up the block," was his reasoning and I

respected it. But I also knew my new siblings would outgrow the space sooner than later, especially since his wife didn't seem to be interested in slowing up on the babymaking any time soon.

Gross.

Doing my best to shake off those thoughts, I was grateful when the doorbell rang, serving as the perfect distraction that reminded me of my own... *not* baby-making. But it did make my pussy jump with anticipation, an unmovable grin on my lips as I pulled the door open and saw Dre's eyebrows bunched in confusion.

Instead of greeting me properly, he asked, "Is Niko Verette your neighbor? Cause I could've sworn I just saw him pull up in a *Tesla.*"

"To which house?" I asked, watching as he pointed out the spot a few doors down with the Barbie pink *Fiat* sitting in the driveway. "Nah, that's where my friend Jayde lives. Remember that EP I had you listen to on our flight to Connecticut?"

"*The honky tonk bullshit?*" he asked, sounding legitimately shocked when he followed, "She's clockin' dollars like that off those country covers?!"

With a laugh, I explained, "She's a songwriter too, and plays instruments, and is just... hella talented overall."

"I was about to say. Shit, in that case, I can croon about whiskey and bad breakups too," he replied with a chuckle that had me shaking my head as I finally invited him in.

Again, because it was something I rarely did, I expected it to feel awkward and different. But it didn't, seeming totally natural for Dre to drop his bag and shoes at the door as I thought out loud, "I wonder what Niko is doing over there, though."

"Probably the same thing I'm about to do over here," Dre answered with the sexiest grin, biting down into his bottom lip as he finally checked me out.

"*Oh yeah?* And what are you about to do over here?" I asked with a smirk, leaning against the wall and crossing my arms in a way that made my titties bunch in the camisole that was just barely holding them in anyway.

Dre seemed to appreciate it though, licking his lips as he pulled me off the wall into a hug and answered, "Make you pay for fuckin' up my ankle."

"It really still hurts?"

Somehow, I knew he was exaggerating when he nodded and whined, "Hell yeah. I mean, I'm walkin'. But it's still a little swollen, and I can feel it ache with every step."

"Old man shit," I teased with a laugh, pulling away from him to head towards the kitchen so that I could offer, "You want some ice?"

"Nah. I want some ass," he growled from behind me, catching up to my stride so that he could give my butt a hard smack that made me jump and giggle all at once.

"The way you talk behind closed doors is just... *whew.* I can't explain it," I sighed, directing him to take a seat at the kitchen island so that I could grab a bottled water from the fridge since his whole demeanor had me feeling especially parched.

I mean, he looked just as good as he did earlier; *just as good as he always did.* But now that he had me alone, his seductive swagger seemed even more activated, sending shivers down my spine when he flat out asked, "Makes your pussy wet?"

"So very wet," I admitted, bending over to grab a water from the bottom shelf and maybe staying down there a second longer than necessary since I could feel Dre's eyes on my ass.

When I turned around to slide a bottle his way out of courtesy, he didn't bother pretending like he hadn't been looking. In fact, he supplied evidence once he asked, "You put those little ass shorts on just for me?"

"The least I could do after crossin' you up earlier. Consider it a sympathy gift," I teased, taking a sip from my bottle as Dre abandoned his to round the corner and pull me into a loose hug.

With his hand just gently resting against my waist, he asked, "I'm never gonna hear the last of that, huh?"

"Not until I get my championship banner. And then you won't be hearing the last of *that*," I replied, speaking it into existence the same way I'd done earlier. And because Dre understood, he only nodded in support of my obsession, tightening his hold on me to address another part of my response.

"You sayin' I'll still be around to listen to you brag?"

Smirking, I quickly fired back, "Ask yourself that question, Jordan Leonard."

"*Jordan Leonard,*" he repeated with a huff of a laugh. "That shit really makes you feel exclusive, huh?

"It absolutely does. Unless that's the fun fact you tell all your women to make them feel like they really know you."

Just the thought had me a little annoyed like I hadn't brought it on myself. And instead of putting me totally at ease about the possibility of others, he only teased, "*Damn.* I see you've peeped my game early."

"Oh, fuck you," I replied with a giggle and a smack to his chest, pulling myself out of his hold so that I could cross the kitchen for no particular reason.

Or maybe there was a reason, Dre taking notice enough to follow me and ask, "Why you keep runnin' away from me like you don't know what you had me come over here for?"

"I'm not running away," I defended, gnawing at my lip as I contemplated sharing the truth I'd been sitting on since that conversation with Ari.

I didn't want Dre to think I was crazy attached, or that I was already trying to make too much out of whatever this was happening between us. But after catching the skeptical look on his face, I realized there was no better time than the present to just be honest, releasing a heavy sigh before I started, "*I just…* okay. This is gonna sound so corny, but I need to get it off my chest so here it goes."

It took another deep breath for me to work up the courage to look him in the eyes when I confessed, "I like you, Dre. And being around you, it makes me feel giddy, and giggly, and I know I had you come over here to blow my back out which we'll get to when I'm done running my mouth. But now that you're here, I can't let this moment pass without telling you that… I like you."

At first he just stared at me, making me nervous until I saw his lips curl up into a grin as he pulled me closer to ask, "That was really hard for you to admit, huh?"

"*Extremely,*" I breathed, not feeling all that relieved about it when he pressed, "But you did it anyway. For me?"

"For you. Well, really for us, *but…*"

Cutting me off with a laugh, he tightened his hug and said, "I don't know how the hell we got here since you used to hate my ass, *but…*"

This time, it was me cutting him off as I corrected, "I never hated you! I actually loved you long before I even knew you. And then I was disappointed, *as a fan*, when you fell off the map. And then I was mad cause, how dare your fine ass pop back up on the scene wanting to coach in our league. And *then…*"

"And then you got to know me and caught feelings," he finished for me, his grin adorably wide when he concluded, "This shit is full circle as hell, Selena."

"Not *quite* full circle, *but…*"

"We'll get there. Cause I like your competitive ass too."

My cheeks grew warm at his profession, a smirk on my lips as I playfully asked, "Oh, you do, huh?"

"Yeah. I do," he stated confidently, giving a little nod as if he was inviting me in for a kiss. And I was happy to give it, relishing in the feel of his lips against mine and his fingers pressed into my ass as he pulled away to whisper, "And now it's time for me to blow your back out."

"Oh my God, Dre," I giggled, quickly getting lost in the kiss he followed up with once he slipped his tongue between my lips and backed me into the kitchen island for leverage. And instead of letting me stay there, he lifted me onto the counter so that we were almost eye-to-eye, my arms wrapped around his neck as he lodged himself between my thighs and nipped at my bottom lip before soothing it with a kiss.

"Where we takin' this, lil' baby?" he asked breathily, dragging his kisses from my lips down to my chin and then over to my neck which he knew would make me weak.

I was grateful that I was already sitting down, though I still held onto his shoulders to keep myself upright as I challenged, "Who said we have to take it anywhere?"

Chuckling right against my neck, his tone sounded especially sultry when he asked, "Oh, that's what you on?"

"We have all night, *and* I can be as loud as I want? You'll be lucky if we don't cover every room in this bitch," I joked, lowkey finding the challenge intriguing now that it was in my head. And that feeling only grew when Dre started tugging at my shorts, getting them down to my ankles for me to kick off before returning to stand between my thighs with a grin on his face as he stared me down like he was contemplating what he wanted to do first.

Between the weight of his dick now pressed against the seat of my panties and the cool counter under my ass cheeks, I felt sensitive all over. And Dre took full advantage of that, pressing lingering kisses against my collarbone then pushing one strap of my camisole from my shoulder for better access to the skin he seemed obsessed with considering the way his mouth refused to let up.

I loved it, though. Loved it so much that I removed the other strap so that he could get everything he was after, his hand resting gently against my throat as he gave equal attention to both sides of my body. And after doing the honors of ridding me of my tank completely, he carried that same balanced energy down to my breasts, instructing me to lay back so he could grab handfuls of each to taste and drive me insane all at once.

I mean, between the warmth of his mouth and the skill of his tongue taunting my nipples before satisfying their craving with a full suck, I felt like I was going to explode. But that seemed to be Dre's goal as he gently urged me further onto the counter so that he could finally get rid of my panties and dive face-first into my pussy with no sort of warning.

Not that it would've mattered.

I was already high, already floating, already over-flowing with arousal that it could've been his dick instead of his mouth and I would've accepted it all the same. But because it was his mouth, I found myself arching up against it, his arms wrapped tightly around my thighs to keep me where he wanted me as he licked, and slurped, and did the type of shit that made me want to make him a stay-at-home husband just so that he could be readily available to do this all the time.

It was... *heavenly*. And because it was heavenly, it only made sense for me to feel like I was rising towards the sky chest first before crashing down hard with an orgasm so intense I felt it everywhere.

My pussy, my toes, my ears, my scalp...

Every part of me felt affected as Dre stood upright with a grin, wiping his mouth with the back of his hand before he said, "One room down. Plenty more to go."

Serving a smirk in response, I took a second to let my limbs regain their strength. Then I climbed down from the counter and pulled him towards the living room, Dre taking a quick detour to grab some protection from his bag by the door which was so very smart on his part since I was all over him once he made it back and would've, *without question*, ignored the "safety first" mantra in favor of getting him inside of me as quickly as possible.

Those seconds of wait time were well worth it though once I found myself in his lap, *on his dick*, my pussy already stretched to accommodate his size when he smacked my ass and urged me to take more. And because I was a glutton for this exact kind of punishment, I did just that, my head tossed back as Dre coached, "There you go, baby. Get that shit. It's yours."

"It's yours," played back in my head as I found my groove, using every bit of strength in my hips and thighs to let him know he'd made a wise decision coming here tonight. But from the look on his face, there was no doubt in his mind that not only had he made a wise decision but that there was also plenty more of where this came from, his hands at my waist like gentle guides when he groaned, *"Fuck yeah."* And just when I thought it couldn't get any better, he brought a hand to the small of my back and used the other to grab my titty, giving my nipple a hard suck that sent me spiraling as I rode him harder, and faster, *and...*

"Shit," we hissed simultaneously, every nerve ending in my body pulsating as I continued to ride him through our shared climax. And by the time I was done, it felt like I'd truly ascended to the promise land, my chest pressed against his as I rested my forehead on his shoulder while he turned to kiss my temple and cheek before whispering into my ear, "Room two. *Check.*"

With a breathy giggle, I admitted, "I might've talked some shit that I can't back up with that one."

"That's aight. Quality over quantity. And besides, if I fucked you in every room tonight, you'd undoubtedly end up on the injury report for next game," he insisted, just the thought of getting sexed to the point of having to call out of work making me tremble as I sat up to respond.

"*I*... can't even dispute that one."

"Oh, I know," he replied with an arrogant chuckle that I couldn't even humble him about because, *well*, he'd earned the rights to that shit.

That wasn't the only thing he'd earned the rights to, my arms wrapped around his neck when I asked, "Should we take this party upstairs? Like, to end it with sleep. Not more of this."

Instead of answering right away, he leaned forward to take a nibble of my collarbone, causing me to involuntarily throb around his dick that was still erect inside of me as we shared a moan before he pointed out, "Your mouth is sayin' one thing, but your pussy is sayin' another. So what's the truth, Ms. Samuels?"

The sexiness in his approach had me second-guessing my plans to call it a night just that easily. And after observing the way he scraped his bottom lip with his teeth like his mind was already made up, I decided I was done holding onto my last thread of control, gnawing into my own lip when I answered, "The truth is... I don't know. But you should grab your bag and follow me upstairs so we can both find out."

I woke up the next morning to kisses against my shoulder blade.

They were gentle, almost feather-like, but still enough to stir something deep in my belly as I slowly rolled over to see the source who somehow looked even better under the sunshine beaming through my window.

Honestly, if this was a decade ago, I would've assumed it was a dream waking up with Dre Leonard in my bed. But after a hard blink that flooded me with vivid memories of last night, I knew it was very real, my voice still groggy when I asked, "Is your fine evolving right before my eyes, or am I just seeing you through dick goggles now?"

Chuckling, he brushed my hair out of my face and replied, "Good morning to you too, lil' baby. How'd you sleep?"

With a yawn I slightly stifled so that I wouldn't blow dragon breath directly into his face, I answered, "I slept so good that I want more of it. Wake me back up in like, twenty minutes." And I was already turning back over when I heard Dre laughing to himself, his weight making the mattress shift before we both settled in for what I expected to be an extra snooze until I heard a video of a woman singing playing from his phone followed by him groaning, "*Well damn.*"

"What?" I asked, flipping right back over so that I could see what had him making so much noise.

Instead of giving an answer right away, he grinned down at me and teased, "I thought you said you wanted to sleep?"

"I did until you started playing that loud ass video and got me all intrigued," I whined, already peeking at the screen to see what I could pull from it on my own as he gave an explanation.

"I was just checking out the latest entries of this *#forthegram* singing competition. Have you heard of it?"

"Of course I've heard of it. And I already have

@Okin4thegram picked to win it all," I told him confidently, recognizing whoever "Okin" was as the only true vocalist in the bunch even though he'd yet to unveil who he was.

Dre wasn't as sure about my pick though, a skeptical look on his face when he countered, "I don't know, Selena. I mean, @Okin4thegram is cold. But that Melina chick has been giving him a run for his money." Then he turned the screen a little more my way to show me that's what had had his attention from the beginning, a video of the girl singing *"Yoga"* by Janelle Monae while doing yoga poses with barely any clothes on.

As far as strategy went, I couldn't knock her game. But because of what the contest was supposed to be about - *vocals, not vagina prints* - I rolled my eyes as I told him, "If Melina was smart, she'd drop out of the contest and make a premium *Snapchat* or an *OnlyFans* account. I'm sure she'd make a killing sharing the exact same shit she's been posting for the competition."

It wasn't a joke, but Dre laughed anyway, scrolling to another entry by someone named John C. that we quickly found ourselves talking over.

"The most competitive person I've ever met is judging somebody for doing whatever it takes to win?"

Shaking my head, I defended, "I'm not judging her at all. I'm just thinking with a business mindset. I mean, most recording contracts are lousy as hell these days anyway. Might as well become an entrepreneur."

Again, my serious observation made Dre laugh as he scrolled to the next entry and said, "Well she ain't the only one playing the game. Check out what your boy @Okin4thegram just posted."

With one glance, I could already tell the video was a

much different vibe than the stuff he'd previously posted, the fact that he was shirtless enough for me to sit up in the bed. And as I watched the video show off his body while he sang, I found myself groaning, *"Well damn"* Dre trying to snap me out of it when he pulled the screen from my view and scolded, "Nah, keep that same energy you had with Melina."

"Dre, quit playin'! Let me see the video," I whined, reaching for his phone as he did his best to block me.

"Nah, you gotta watch this shit with your eyes closed or somethin'."

"Dre, come on, " I giggled, wrestling my way on top of him and locking his arm in a way that left him no choice but to let me see it. And now that I was viewing it for a second time, I noticed new things, my eyes squinted when I commented, "This background looks so familiar to me."

"Aight, aight. That's enough," he rattled, launching the phone towards the end of the mattress with the video still playing as I straddled his lap and laughed in his face.

"Are you really gettin' jealous? I don't even know who that dude is!"

"But if you had on panties, I bet he would've sung them right off," he fired back with a scowl, only making me laugh harder as I put my finger to my chin and sang, *"Hmm…* I wonder how they got off in the first place…"

"Do you need a reminder?" he asked, his hands finding their rightful place on my ass for a squeeze that had me gnawing into my lip as I battled between my wants and needs.

Yes, I *wanted* a reminder. But did I *need* it?

As if it was answering the question for me, my

stomach growled with perfect timing, its volume border-line embarrassing as I told Dre, "No. I *need* some food."

He wasn't giving up though, his dick already rock hard between us when he suggested, "Maybe a snack and then a reminder?"

"A meal, and then a nap, and *then* a reminder," I laid out, climbing out of his lap to let him know I was serious about my plans as I got up to stretch. And thankfully, Dre didn't fight me on it - *cause he might've won* - going with the flow of our lazy day off that was damn near perfect until my father interrupted with a phone call about his Fourth of July cookout coming up.

"I know you're in the middle of the season, but you can make a little time for your father, right?"

"The same way you make so much time for me?" I thought to myself with a sarcastic roll of my eyes, Dre watching me intently as I told my father, "Yes, Daddy. I can."

"I've been working on this new sauce recipe, even though you know my meat don't need no damn sauce. But anyway, Darla loves it!" he exclaimed, just the mention of her making me even more annoyed when I plainly replied, "I'm sure she does, Daddy."

Apparently, I'd kept it a little *too* plain, my father picking up on my attitude enough to ask, "Everything alright Selena?"

With a nod he couldn't see, I sighed, "Yes, I'm fine. I just… today is one of very few days off during the season, so I'm trying to relax as much as possible."

That was only partially true, the other part of it a conversation I knew I wasn't interested in having today. And I was grateful my father knew not to press me on it, offering a somber, "I understand," before picking his voice back up to say, "Well let me get out of your hair. I'll see you for the holiday. Love you, baby girl."

"Love you too, Daddy," I replied, ending the call and releasing another sigh that had Dre quick to ask, "You good?"

Nodding, I did my best to brush off the tension from that simple conversation as I answered, "Yeah. That was just my father calling to talk about his new BBQ sauce."

"Sounds like typical dad shit. I mean, at least what I saw them do on TV."

It was subtle. But the reminder of Dre growing up without his father made me feel like a brat for being so awkward with mine, giving me an idea that I blurted before I could change my mind. "He invited me over for the holiday coming up. You should come with me."

"Come with you?" he asked, clearly surprised by the invitation. And because I didn't want things to be awkward with him too, I tried to take some of the pressure off when I responded.

"Not like as my date. But just for support or whatever."

I expected him to, *at least*, contemplate the idea, give some thought to what being seen with me would mean, weigh the pros and cons of sharing a meal with a bunch of Nashville locals who had cheered his rise and judged his fall. But he didn't do any of that, only kissed my cheek before telling me, "If that's what you want, Selena."

As far as the cookout went, it was *exactly* what I wanted. But as far as my life went, it was starting to seem like Dre's cool and calm demeanor was maybe what I needed.

TWELVE

SOME GOOD FOOD was exactly what I needed to balance out the bit of anxiety that came with joining Selena for her father's Fourth of July cookout.

As far as everyone here knew, I was just tagging along because I didn't have any other plans for the day and Selena knew there'd be plenty of food. But that still didn't mean I felt totally at ease; especially since I hadn't accounted for the lingering stares I'd get from her uncles and cousins who'd all apparently been huge fans of mine before I was ousted from the league, her father being the only one willing to actually speak on it when he commented, "Man, if I was you, I'd rock that championship ring everywhere I went! You wouldn't be able to take it off of me!"

With a chuckle, I wiped my BBQ sauce-covered fingers on a napkin and told him, "To be honest, I've barely even worn it.

"What? Why not?!" he asked hysterically, damn near flying out of his patio chair as Selena reached over to calm him down with a hand to his forearm and quietly scolded, *"Daddy, mind your business."*

While I appreciated her trying to be protective of my complicated story, I was quick to tell her, "Nah, it's cool, Selena," releasing a heavy sigh before I finally answered, "After the last game of the finals, I found out my grandmother passed. And by the time the ring ceremony rolled around the following season, I was barely present enough to appreciate it since it represented something I still wasn't quite ready to accept; that while I was bustin' my ass for that ring, she was taking her last breaths."

Now that the information was out there, I could see the uncomfortable look on everyone's faces, Darla being the first one to break the tension when she stood up with Selena's brother in her arms and announced, *"I'm...* gonna go put the baby down for his nap."

"Let me come with you, babe. Tell my boy sweet dreams," Selena's father followed, pushing out of his chair to excuse himself for what I knew was less about the baby's nap and more about taking a break from the heaviness of my response.

Honestly, I was fine with that, glad to have it out instead of always keeping it bottled in. Though that didn't stop Selena from leaning over my way to say, "Dre, I'm so sorry about that."

Shaking my head, I told her, "Don't be. I'm good, really. People seem to understand me better when they know the full truth."

Nodding to agree, she added a little smirk when she asked, "Well you know you're like his best friend now, right? I mean, I'm gettin' *all* the cool points around here for bringing a Trojans legend to the cookout."

Because she was so obviously trying to lighten the mood, I joined in, cocking my head to tease, "Damn. So I'm the first? Your boy Kage might feel a way that I beat him to it."

"Oh, shut up!" she squealed with a smack to my arm that didn't slow me down.

"I'm just sayin'. He's probably warming up his *Twitter* fingers as we speak."

"Will you stop?" she half-giggled half-whined, making me chuckle too as I told her, "Nah, I'm just fuckin' with you. Ain't nobody worried about that lil' nigga with the pornstar name."

Snapping her head back, she repeated, "*Pornstar name?* Kage Steele is… *oh my God*, it *does* kinda sound like a pornstar name!"

Of course she'd yelled it just loud enough to draw a few eyes from her other family members congregated in the backyard. But thankfully, they were also in the middle of an intense game of dominoes which meant the attention didn't last long, a frown on my lips as I groaned, "I still can't believe his ass put my mugshot on a t-shirt. Like, what would make him even think to do some stupid shit like that?"

"I don't know, but I kinda want one now," Selena admitted, waiting until I snapped my eyes her way to add, "Not from him, and not to wear in public. But just to have, as a keepsake."

"You better not," I warned, catching the challenging look of, "*What are you gonna do about it*" already brewing in Selena's eyes as her father returned to his seat and changed the subject.

"So when's your next game, baby girl?"

Averting her eyes like she had to think about it, she

used her fingers to list, "We fly to Atlanta tomorrow for a game the day after. And then we go to Chicago for a game before coming back to play Phoenix here at home."

"Okay, okay. I'll be at the Phoenix game then," her father replied as he pulled out a damn pocket calendar, tempting me to laugh until I saw the legitimately shocked expression on Selena's face when she asked, *"You will?"*

With an easy nod, he was already flipping to this month when he answered, "Yeah. I know I haven't been able to make it to any so far this season, but I miss watching you play in person."

"And I miss seeing you in the crowd, Daddy," Selena gushed, her grin wide and her doe eyes looking even bigger than usual as she looked on the verge of happy tears.

Because of who Selena was, she didn't let them fall though, just smiling on as her father shared, "I remember when Selena couldn't stand having me at her games. *"Stop yelling, Daddy!"*, *"You aren't the coach, Daddy!"*, *"I can't shoot every shot, Daddy!"* Now look at you. My have the tides turned."

With a dramatic roll of her eyes, Selena groaned, *"Anyway.* I'll be sure to leave some tickets at Will Call for you and your family."

"Our family, Selena," her father corrected, reaching to give her hand a squeeze that Selena seemed to appreciate once she quietly agreed.

"Yeah, that too."

The whole thing was touching as hell to witness; especially knowing the backstory of their relationship since, according to Selena, this was who they'd been before when it was just the two of them. So to see them making baby steps in the right direction was *inspiring* to say the least; though that inspiration was destroyed almost instantly when I checked my phone to find a text I'd received over an hour ago from an old friend and neighbor back in St. Louis.

"Your mother is having another episode outside of the house." - Porscha

"Did you try to talk to her?" - Dre

Doing my best to rejoin the conversation with Selena and her father, I gave nods when appropriate in regard to how the season had been going so far. But it was still hard to focus, even more so when I finally received a response.

"Of course I did, but she's on one." - Porscha

"No surprise," I thought, keying out the only response that made sense since there was really nothing else I could do about it from here in Nashville.

"Call the police." - Dre

"In this climate?! Are you crazy?!" - Porscha

I hated how right she was, knowing just how easily a simple trespassing call involving my unstable mother could turn into the unthinkable with the police involved. And because I really had no other choice since there was no one I trusted to handle the situation, I decided I'd just have to make the trip, letting Porscha know that when I replied, **"I'll be there as soon as I can."** before breaking the news to the Samuels.

Clearing my throat, I interrupted their conversation to announce, "I hate to dash early, but I have somethin' I need to go handle."

While Selena was already giving me a look of concern in response, her father was completely chill when he offered, "No worries, son. It was great having you over." Then he pulled out his phone to say, "Baby girl, get a picture of me and DeAndre so I can show all my *Facebook* friends," standing up and moving to my side of the table to pose before requesting, "Okay, okay. Now let me get one of you two together."

"Daddy, don't post this one on *Facebook*. I don't wanna start any rumors," Selena insisted as she moved to my side, my arm already tossed over her shoulder when I bent to whisper in her ear, "Are they really rumors though?"

"Shut up, Dre," she replied through her smile, her father taking enough pictures to make an album of before sending me to say goodbye to everyone else which turned into even more pictures.

Because it was better than the stares they'd given me

earlier, I rolled with it, saving my most important goodbye for last after Selena volunteered to walk me to my car. And though I could still feel the concern surrounding my abrupt exit in her demeanor, I did my best to put her at ease when I smiled to say, "I'll see you later, Ms. Samuels. Thanks again for the invite."

"You sure you don't wanna take a plate to-go?" she asked, catching my car door once I opened it to climb in.

"Yeah, I'm sure. I'm not going straight home, and I don't want my whip smelling like BBQ."

"Well be safe. *Wherever you're headed*," she said with a sigh that told me she was struggling not to bombard me with questions.

I appreciated her efforts, but I also knew there was nothing I really wanted her to worry about. So instead of even putting anything specific in her mind to be concerned with, I simply replied, "I'll explain everything later, okay?"

"Yeah, aight," she muttered with a subtle roll of her eyes that had me groaning her name. And this time, she seemed to mean it when she said, "Okay, okay. I heard you, Dre. Later," heading back to the house and leaving me to figure out my exact move.

Flying would've been the smart thing to do, but it was also the thing I hated most. And since I really wasn't interested in handling the logistics of that anyway, I decided to hit the road for the almost five-hour drive that I'd done more times than I cared to count.

It was almost midnight when I pulled up to my grandmother's house to find my mother passed out in the chair on the front porch. It was the same chair my grandmother used to watch over the entire block from and the chair I refused to move even after all these years as if she'd ever be back to sit in it.

"I'd do anything to see her sitting in this chair again," I thought to myself with a heavy sigh, staring hard at the person who *was* sitting in it with a mix of emotions.

Anger, disappointment, and annoyance were just a few. But instead of letting my feelings get involved, I decided to be tactical when I gave her shoulder a shake and demanded, "Jeri, get up."

Because of whatever substance that had brought her here in the first place, it took a minute for her to really respond, her eyes bloodshot red when they finally cracked open to see who was disturbing her. And once she realized it was me, she gave a smile that was missing a few more teeth than the last time we spoke, her voice especially raspy when she said, "Oh hey, baby. I didn't know you were in town."

Instead of letting her take the conversation some-where else, I stayed on the topic at hand when I reminded her, "Jeri, you know you ain't supposed to be anywhere near here, so what are you doin'?"

Frowning, she sat up a little straighter - *and wobbled in the process* - before wagging her finger my way to respond, "What do you mean, what am I doin'? This is my moth-er's house! This is where I grew up! I can be here!"

Now that she called herself getting loud with me, I knew I didn't have much time before she caused another scene, keeping my voice as leveled as possible when I told her, "You gotta go, man."

Of course that only seemed to rile her up even more

as she popped up from her seat and stumbled while shouting, "She was my mother! Not yours, Dre! Mine!"

"Well she was more of a mother to me than you could've ever been!" I snapped, more mad at myself for letting this situation take me there than I was at her for being, *well*, her.

I mean, I really hadn't even come here to fight with her; just to make sure that she didn't do anything crazy and that my grandmother's house remained in the same condition. But I shouldn't have been surprised that it turned into this, my mother bursting into tears as she confessed, "Dre baby, I'm so sorry. I'm so sorry. I just miss her. I miss her so much. I miss her every day."

"Yeah, I do too," I replied quietly, my heart growing heavy as I stared at the now empty chair wondering how different things could've been if she hadn't left us all those years ago.

Would my mother have eventually gotten the help she needed?

Would I still be in the league?

Would we finally be functioning like a normal family instead of this shit show I was dealing with now?

As if she could read my mind, my mother started reminiscing on one of our few "normal" moments from the past, leaning against one of the porch's posts to ask, "Remember on the fourth when she'd always yell at me for bringing you a round of black cats to set off?"

Because it was one of very few fond memories I had with my mother from my childhood and one of the few things I knew I could always look forward to as far as her inconsistent visits went throughout the year, it was hard not to grin a little when I answered, "Yeah, I remember."

"But I'd do it anyway. Because you loved them," she

said with a grin of her own, glaring up at the sky to watch the fireworks still going off in the neighborhood as she brought up another memory. "And remember when you chased your grandma with that bag of snappers I bought you? Your little bad ass kept throwing them right at her feet!"

"I didn't even know grandma could move like that," I told her with a little chuckle, thinking back on the ass whooping I got once my bag of snappers was finally empty.

It was the kind of whooping that pretty much kept me in check for the rest of my childhood, though I really couldn't do much wrong in my grandmother's eyes anyway. I was her baby. And because of my situation with my parents, I knew she felt kind of sorry for me, wanting to put me in the best situation she possibly could so that I wouldn't fail solely because of their short-comings.

Little did she know, I'd be the cause of my own demise. Though my mother somehow saw it differently enough to comment, "You look like you've been taking better care of yourself. That's good. I'm glad to see you doing good."

As far as the last five or so years went, I was defi-nitely in a better place than I had been. But one look at her only reminded me of those not-so-good times, a frown on my face when I replied, "Wish I could say the same about you, Jeri."

Shaking her head, she sighed, "Lord knows I'm tryin'. Every day is a struggle. Every. *Single*. Day."

Strangely enough, that was something we could relate on; the daily struggle of making sure your reasons to stay clean continuously outweighed the desire for a tiny hit. But lucky for me, I had plenty of things going on to stay busy and motivated, something I knew I couldn't say for her since she was right where she'd always been.

Well, at least to some degree, my eyebrows bunched when I asked, "Where are you staying at now?"

Shrugging, she answered, "Oh, you know. A little bit of everywhere."

I knew that was code for her essentially being homeless, something my heart couldn't allow no matter how much wrong she'd done. And since it was already late, I made an executive decision for us both to get some rest, offering her hand as I said, "Come on. Let's go inside. Get you cleaned up."

For whatever reason, my simple invitation brought tears to her eyes, her dainty hand squeezing my much larger one as I unlocked the door to my grandmother's house. And once I stepped inside, I was hit with a rush of emotions, taking me back to the months I'd spent holed up here questioning my existence long after my grandmother passed and long before Mr. Lloyd showed up.

That's when it all really spiraled out of control; the anxiety, the paranoia, the addiction. But to honor her legacy in this moment, I knew I had to stay strong, putting on a brave face as my mother whispered, "I think it's time, Dre. For us both to let go of this place. It's the only way we can really move forward with our lives. Otherwise, we'll *just…* keep coming back. I'll just keep coming back."

Looking down at her, I couldn't believe what she was suggesting. But after another beat, I knew she was right. While this place represented so much of who I was, was the place I'd called home for so many years and the place we'd both been raised in, the life of it left with my grandmother's spirit and the memories it held now weren't happy for either of us.

The last time I was here, I felt hopeless, like I couldn't trust anyone, like I didn't want to live. And that *just...* wasn't my life anymore.

It couldn't be my life anymore.

Of course there were a few things we both wanted to keep; photo albums, random trinkets, etc. But in that moment, my mother and I made a mutual decision to spend the next few days sorting through what we wanted and making plans to get rid of the rest so that we could finally put the house on the market.

So that we could both finally be free.

THIRTEEN

IT WAS TAKING everything in me not to blow up his phone.

With every day that passed, every game he missed, I found myself growing more and more worried, trying to let his vague texts about *"being okay"* hold me over until he came back from… wherever he was.

The fact that he was keeping it all a secret bothered me. Even when I asked Kat if she had any idea, she only gave me information that I already knew.

"He's handling a personal matter."

Personal matter, my ass.

My concern for his well-being was beginning to override my performance on the court, and that was a problem.

I mean, it was no one's fault but my own for growing so attached so quickly, for caring so much about him, for admitting that I liked him and inviting him to meet my father even if it wasn't like that.

The optics said otherwise.

Dre going with the flow and being cool about my father's antics said otherwise.

But that was also the last time I'd seen Dre. So hell, maybe that said something too.

Had I scared him off to the point that he didn't even feel comfortable showing up to his job?

No, that was ridiculous. I knew what coaching for the Nymphs meant to Dre, and he wouldn't blow that opportunity for anyone; not even me. But the fact that he'd now missed three games straight and no one knew what was really going on with him…

Shaking my head, I did my best to focus my attention back on Sugar's postgame speech, listening in as she announced, "That game was a hot mess, so let's just focus on the good of our very own Selena Samuels being voted as an All-Star!"

Wait, what?

Before I could really process the information, my teammates were already crowding me in celebration, Mikayla's voice somehow being the only one I could hear when she shouted, "I know that's right, Sharpshooter!"

Accepting their praise, I gave as many "thank yous" as I could before Sugar asked everyone to settle down so that she could share more information. But once she announced that I'd also been selected to participate in this year's Three-Point Shootout and that Mikayla had been picked to participate in the Skills Challenge, all hell broke loose like we hadn't just lost a game, the whole locker room cheering as someone started playing music from their *Bluetooth* speaker that Sugar shut down immediately.

"*Nu uh!* Did y'all forget what just happened out there

tonight?! We still have games before All-Star, and we sure as hell have plenty more after it so stay focused!" she shouted at the team before directing her attention to just Mikayla and I to say, "Congratulations, you two. Enjoy this huge honor and the weekend in Vegas when it comes. But don't forget what our team goal is for this season."

"I got you, Coach," I told her with a confident nod, completely tuned in as she gave a rundown of our schedule for the rest of the week before dismissing us to do postgame stuff. And of course, now that the All-Star announcement had been made, all the questions I received were about that, making it a little easier on me since that meant I didn't have to talk as much about my poor play tonight.

My poor play because of... *well*, not because of him since I was the one out there on the court; not him. But still, his absence affected me and that was something I needed to process, wondering if being involved with Dre was even worth the trouble if it equated to feeling like this.

The fact that the moment was still in progress certainly didn't help my cause, giving me every reason to call it a wash the second I knew he was okay. But because I didn't know for sure, I stayed worried, and I continued to check my phone, and I stalked his social media for clues even though I knew he wasn't all that active on it.

Even when my doorbell rang to signal my food order had arrived, I kept my phone in my hand, not wanting to miss anything when I pulled it open and saw it... *wasn't my food*.

It was him.

"*Dre…*" I sighed, more relieved than anything to see him in one piece. And you would've thought he hadn't gone ghost at all considering the way he smirked to tease, "I heard an All-Star lives here. Is that true? And if so, can I get her autograph?"

With a roll of my eyes, I pulled the door open to let him inside, waiting until it was closed behind us to ask, "Where the hell have you been, Dre?!"

"It's a long story, Selena," he answered with a sigh, scrubbing a hand down his face when he added, "I didn't want you to worry."

"Well congratulations, I did anyway! Like, a lot. And I've been playing shitty because of it," I whined as if I hadn't already come to terms with that part of it being my fault.

Still, he needed to hear about it. And it made me feel a little better when he wrapped me in a low hug to say, "I'm sorry, lil' baby. But that's why I'm here now. To explain what's been goin' on."

"I'm listening," I replied with more attitude than I felt since being in his arms always made it hard for me to think straight. And thankfully, I didn't have to stay there, the ringing of the doorbell snapping me out of the trance I was slowly falling into as I pushed myself out of his hold to explain, "It's the food I thought you were."

Instead of letting me handle it, Dre opened the door to get it himself. And because the order was under my latest alias, Patricia - *don't ask* - , the delivery guy was beyond surprised to see him, literally shaking as he handed over my chicken alfredo, Caesar salad and cheesecake from 12 South Bistro.

"Appreciate you, bro. Have a good night," Dre told

him with a polite nod, already closing the door in his face as the guy stammered, *"You...* you too, Mr. Leonard." And after locking the door behind him, Dre carried the food to my kitchen like he just owned the place - *and the food* - already unbagging it for me on the kitchen island as he started his story.

"Aight, so... after I left the cookout at your father's house, I drove to St. Louis."

"You drove to St. Louis?" I repeated, my eyes tight with confusion as he pushed the salad my way to eat first like he just knew that's what I wanted.

It was what I wanted. And once he slid the plastic fork my way, I dug right in, not even bothered by the pre-dressed lettuce as I listened to Dre explain, "Since my grandmother passed, my mother randomly has these episodes outside of her house; usually because of what-ever she's been smoking or drinking. She'll be in the yard screaming, and crying, and *just...* having a big ass, dramatic meltdown."

My heart was already aching for a number of reasons, but I stayed quiet, balancing my attention between Dre and the salad as he continued, "Thank-fully, the neighbors know to alert me when it happens instead of just calling the police even though this last one, I kinda wanted them to. But I'm glad they didn't cause by the time I got there, my mother had sobered up enough to have a long-overdue conversation about what to do with my grandmother's estate."

Because I knew how much his grandmother meant to him and what role his mother played in her passing, I had tons of questions about how they'd even gotten to the point of speaking. But it wasn't my business to pry in quite yet, letting him get it all out when he sighed to finish, "So that's why I've been away. We cleaned out the house, got it put on the market, and now we're just waiting for a buyer."

Nodding, I shoved a bite of salad in my mouth before asking, "Your mother. Is she okay?"

The way he sort of shrugged and chuckled in response had me confused until he explained, "Honestly, it's a daily thing with her. Damn near an hourly thing. But we got her somewhere safe to stay temporarily until the house sales, and then we're gonna use some of that money to put her in a nicer, long-term rehab facility."

It sounded like a great plan, one I was glad they'd agreed on even with their relationship being rocky. But because it wasn't like him to hide much from me no matter how complicated, I also couldn't help asking, "Dre, why didn't you just tell me? I would've come with you, or at least come to help."

Even with my busy schedule, there were pockets of time I could've made to be supportive of him the same way he'd done for me. But he didn't exactly agree with that logic, rounding the island to take the barstool next to mine and reply, "It wasn't your problem to deal with, Selena. This was something I needed to do on my own so that I could come back to the city free; so I could come back to you open."

Now that I knew the ins and outs of what he'd been up to all this time - *trying to get his personal endeavors in order not only to benefit him but also to benefit us* - I felt silly when I admitted, "I thought you might've relapsed."

"*What?*"

Dropping my fork, I turned his way to explain, "You were being so vague, didn't wanna talk on the phone or *FaceTime*, went missing on both me *and* the team with a *"personal matter"*. I thought maybe you had fell back on old habits."

From the look on his face, I could tell he was a little disappointed that that was where my thought process had taken me to. And in an effort to help him better understand how I got there, I was quick to add, "I also thought I had scared you off by introducing you to my father, so I pretty much exhausted every possible explanation for you being away."

The little laugh he let out made me feel a bit better even though it was paired with a frown when he asked, "*Wait*. Why would I trip off meeting your dad?"

"I don't know," I whined, gnawing at my lip as I pushed out, "I was just pressed for an answer because I care about you, Dre. I care about you a lot. I care about you as my friend, as my coach, as the only person who can show up to my house in the middle of the night and not get sent away for not texting or calling first…"

"Your greedy ass only opened the door cause you thought I was your food," he interrupted with a smirk, reaching for my cheesecake until I slapped his hand.

"That's not the point, Dre. The point is, your well-being matters to me. And I don't know how I feel about that if it means playing more games like today and spending more nights like this worried sick about you."

It might've sounded a little selfish. But considering how new things were with us, it would've been stupid of me to knowingly set myself up for a dynamic I didn't want, Dre not exactly making me feel much better about it when he grabbed my hand to say, "Selena, I can't make any promises cause I honestly don't know what's gonna happen. None of us do. But I need you to trust me when I tell you not to worry."

"Easier said than done; especially considering your history," I sighed, watching as Dre's face almost immediately scrunched into a frown.

"My history with you, or my life history? Cause I know good and well I haven't given you any reason to be suspicious about if I'm telling you the truth or not. But if you're always gonna hold my past shit against me, I can save us both the time and just leave now."

The way he said it made my chest tight, letting me know I was already in a lot deeper than I was talking. Sure, "us" being a thing was new, but my feelings for Dre weren't new at all. And they were honestly a little hurt until he grabbed my chin and expressed, "Look, Selena. I want this. If I didn't, I wouldn't have shown up tonight fresh off the road; would've just caught you at practice tomorrow with everyone else. But your well-being matters to me too. I care about you too."

I would've been lying if I didn't admit how much his words softened my stance, how much his touch softened me period. And honestly, the longer I looked into his eyes, the more I believed him; though I purposely pulled away from his hold and returned my attention to my salad when I asked, "Just don't ever do that to me again, okay?"

Popping up from his seat, he moved so that he could drape himself around me from behind and speak right into my ear. "I'm fuckin' with an All-Star now. You think I'd purposely drop that ball?"

"I *am* an All-Star, huh?" I bragged with a smirk, turning my face a little to share, "I also got picked to do the Three-Point Shootout which means we have some work to do in the gym."

If there was anyone I could count on to get me right

for a shooting competition, it was Coach Leonard. Though apparently, that was the last thing on his mind when he went full Dre and countered, "As long as we're good. That's what matters most."

I appreciated his focus, but I also couldn't help turning around to face him completely when I asked, "Are *you* good? I mean, after going back to your hometown. I know that couldn't have been easy."

It was a tidbit he'd shared on the first day we met; that being back in St. Louis wasn't good for him. And now that I knew so much more about his complicated relationship with the city, I understood why, again wishing I could've been there with him once he answered, "At first, it wasn't. Being back in my grandmother's house, that shit was honestly painful. But now I feel like I can really move forward with my life. And I hope that includes you."

"*Whew*. Come through with the flattery," I teased with a smirk, playfully fanning myself until Dre caught my hands with a serious expression on his face.

"I'm serious, Selena. I've always trusted you with the ball in your hands. But can I do the same with my heart?"

The question gave me butterflies, my heart racing as Dre stared at me waiting for an answer. And honestly, my response didn't take much thinking, my grin tripling in size once I told him, "As long as I can do the same with mine."

"I got you," he replied with a confident nod that told me he held the responsibility in high regard, bending to press a lingering kiss against my forehead before returning to his seat. And now that we'd gotten that perfectly mushy moment out of the way, I

ALEXANDRA WARREN

couldn't wait to comment on his choice of words
regardless of how sweet they were, already laughing
to myself when I picked up my fork and called
him out.

"Dre, you saw me air ball a buzzer-beater. Why on
earth would you trust me with the ball in my hands?" I
asked as I poked around what was left of my salad.

Shrugging, he leaned into the island so that he could
see my eyes when he assured me, "That was a fluke. I
know you got it next time."

"Hopefully, there won't be a next time," I muttered
more to myself than him, just the thought giving me a
bit of anxiety since the last thing I wanted was two
blown games on my record.

Of course Dre saw it differently, completely optimistic when he asked, "You don't want a chance to
redeem yourself?"

Like him, I shrugged. "I mean, if I have to. But I'd
rather just be winning without the pressure of having to
make a last shot."

My preference sounded like a no-brainer to me. And
I was grateful that instead of challenging me on it any
further, Dre nodded to agree. "That's fair. But if it
comes, I need you ready, lil' baby."

Because I didn't even want to speak another
moment like that into existence, I didn't really respond
to his request, only smirking when I peeked his way to
reply, "And I need you ready to make me cum,
big baby."

With the days he'd spent away, my body was definitely missing its dose of Dre, in desperate need of some
real relief after all the worrying I'd done behind him.
But now that he knew he was *at least* back in my good

178

graces, he couldn't help himself in teasing, "I'm only doin' that if you share some of this dessert."

"*Wowww*. So I gotta pay to get some play? Even after you had me all stressed out?"

Chuckling, he reached for my cheesecake once again and answered, "I told you not to worry, lil' baby. But I can't even fake, it's kinda cute that you were."

"Well I'm glad something about me is, cause my stats from tonight weren't cute at all," I groaned with a slow roll of my eyes, not even feeling deserving of the slice of cheesecake Dre was already popping the to-go container top off of when he asked, "That bad, huh?"

"*The worst*. In a double-digit loss that I'm kinda happy my father flaked out on cause it was just that awful of a performance."

So many missed shots.

So many blown plays on defense.

So many turnovers.

There was nothing about it I wanted to remember, so I was glad to hear when Dre decided, "In that case, I guess I can make you feel a lil' better."

"Just a little?" I pressed, knowing I needed much more than that; especially now that he'd already stolen what would've been his replacement – *the cheesecake*.

Sneaking a taste with his fork, he chuckled, "*Damn*. You just greedy all around, huh?"

"Closed mouths don't get fed," I told him with a smirk and a shrug that had him watching me intently with a smile on his face before he blurted something I didn't even realize I cared to hear.

"I missed you."

It hit me right in the chest; soothing and flat-tering me all at once, though I still found room to joke,

"What parts of me specifically? Cause I could use the ego boost."

He didn't even hesitate to gas me up, an instant smile on my lips as he listed, "I missed your wit. And your ass. And your voice. And watching you ball. And did I already say your ass?"

"If you really missed it, you should kiss it, Jordan Leonard," I suggested with a playful side eye that had Dre leaning my way so that he could speak straight into my ear.

"I'm thinkin' about doin' a whole lot more than just kissin' it, Selena Samuels. But I need you to eat first cause I'm sure you haven't been eating enough if you've really been as worried about me as you said you were."

Giggling, I stabbed at the last bit of my salad and replied, "You're cute. But you aren't *"miss meals cause I'm so worried about you"* cute."

"Wowww, that's fucked up," he groaned with a chuckle that told me he wasn't seriously upset about it.

But even if he was, I knew my position, shrugging when I replied, "Lil' baby's gotta eat so she can have the energy to play ball and keep these lights on. But I *did* miss you, though. And I'm really happy you're back, big baby."

While he had let me get away with it the first time, this time he was quick to correct, "I ain't no baby."

"But you're *my* baby," I gushed, moving from my seat to discard the empty salad container in the trash as Dre casually asked a question I should've saw coming.

"Oh, so you claimin' me now?"

"*I mean…*" I sighed, gnawing into the corner of my lip as he firmly stated, "It wasn't a lie. I'm definitely yours, Selena."

His words gave me the same feeling as watching fresh honey hit a warm biscuit, so damn satisfying that I couldn't help but grin as I moved to stand between his legs and challenged, "My big baby?"

"I don't know about all that, *but…*"

Chuckling, I wrapped my arms around his neck. "Well what do you wanna be then?"

"Your man," he stated plainly, leaving no room for misunderstanding even though I still squinted to ask, "That's not the same thing?"

"I'm just making sure you know," he replied as he moved his hands to claim a little something of his own - *my ass*.

With his firm grip, I was happy to confirm, "Oh, *I* know."

"*Good*. Now hurry up and finish your dinner so your man can make you feel better."

"My who?" I asked playfully, not quite ready to extract myself from his hold.

That feeling only grew as I watched him do a slow lick of his lips before he growled, "You heard me, Selena," leaning forward to seal it with a kiss that told me if he wasn't my man already, he certainly was now.

What that meant as far as the public went, I wasn't quite sure. But right now, I wasn't so concerned with that, taking full advantage of our current privacy as I decided to delay the rest of my dinner in favor of slipping my tongue between my man's lips.

FOURTEEN

I WAS UNBELIEVABLY proud of her.

Technically, I was in Las Vegas for work purposes, invited to join Sugar who'd been selected to coach in the All-Star game because of our team's current first place standing in the Eastern conference. But my duties as a coach came second to being happy for Selena as I watched her take on the media, doing a mix of interviews with the most joyous smile on her face like she was completely in her element; because she *was* in her element.

When it came to this shit, being a superstar was her natural state, even in a room filled with the other top players in the league. And because of that, it was hard not to stare obsessively, my gaze trained her way until Sugar snuck up next to me and said, "It was written in the cards, Coach Leonard. Watching you watch her is like déjà vu."

With a nod, I agreed, "Yeah, she's been ballin' her ass off all season. She deserves this moment."

Shaking her head, Sugar crossed her arms over her

chest and leaned a little closer to whisper, "I'm not talking about basketball, Dre. I'm talking about you two finally becoming a thing."

Internally, I panicked. But outwardly, I cued up the answer Selena and I had decided was best to give people until the season was over, trying to sound completely chill when I told Sugar, "We aren't a…"

"Oh, cut the bullshit," she interrupted with a wave of her hand. "No need to hide from me. I mean, hell, ain't like y'all have been tryna hide a damn thing when you two stay up all night knockin' boots after every away game."

"*Hold up*. You've heard us?" I asked, smacking myself when I realized that I'd outed us with my response. And once I saw the smirk on Sugar's face, I had another realization, cocking my head to ask, "And you're really just now sayin' somethin' about it?"

Shrugging, she answered, "If a man has someone in his bedroom and that someone isn't me, then what he's doing in there is not my business to speak on."

Because I could appreciate her take on it, I responded with a nod that had her comfortable enough to continue, "You two seem to have a really special bond, though. Like a real friendship, with a hot sex cherry on top."

"*Sugar…*" I groaned, refusing to go down that route even when she defended, "It's a compliment, Dre! Take it."

I didn't take it. But I didn't *not* take it either, staying quiet as we both watched Selena do her thing. And honestly, I could've stayed there all day, completely content even when Sugar commented, "Look at her, Dre. She's such a star. Consider yourself lucky."

With another nod, I agreed. "Beyond lucky, Coach Daniels."

It wasn't lost on me that Selena could literally have any man she wanted; a fact I didn't take lightly when it came to making sure she was well taken care of even though Sugar was quick to balance things out once she added, "She's lucky too, cause it's not easy to find someone who just… *gets it*. But she's got that in you. You're her someone, Dre."

Turning Sugar's way, I asked, "You think so?"

This time, it was her nodding. "I know so. I mean, the girl knows I'm no threat, and she's still shooting daggers my way with her eyes mid-interview like I want your young ass," she replied with a chuckle that had me peeking in Selena's direction just in time to catch a flash of what Sugar was talking about. "Y'all have fun out here, okay? Not too much fun cause that could cause *major* problems. But enjoy this. Together."

Now that the secret was out, I decided to own it when I replied, "We will." But once I heard someone ask, *"We who?"* I wished I hadn't been so loose, turning over my shoulder to see my boss with a scowl on her face.

"Kat…" I sighed as she held up her hand to interrupt, "Dre, don't tell me y'all were talking about what I think y'all were talking about."

Before I could even respond, Sugar knocked her hand down and scolded, "Kat, leave those folks alone. They aren't hurting anybody."

"Sugar, you know I have a lot of respect for you. But this is something I need you to stay out of, especially considering I've already given firm warnings to both parties involved," Kat replied sharply, shooting a side eye my way that made me roll my eyes as Sugar offered a defense.

"Well they still found their way to each other anyway, so now what? I mean, you really think your little warnings reign over true love?" Sugar asked, my eyes wide when I muttered, *"True love?"* as Kat brushed the whole thing off with a wave of her hand.

"Oh, please. They are *not* in love. Selena's just lonely, and Dre is just... *there*, all the time."

For as much talking as I'd let Sugar do on my behalf, this one I couldn't let her handle, moving closer to Kat to snarl, "You got a lot of nerve speakin' on some shit you know absolutely nothin' about. And even though it's really none of your business, let me put you up on game. Selena and I are together now, and we've already decided to keep it lowkey until the season is over so ain't shit for you to worry about, aight?"

Surprisingly enough, Kat was stunned to silence as Sugar chuckled, "I guess he *told* you," bumping me in the arm to add, "Well done, Dre." And that was enough to snap Kat out of it, a stiff finger pointed my way as she gave what I assumed was a final warning.

"If one word of this gets out to the press, I am on y'all asses. Understood?"

"If it makes you feel better, sure," I answered with a shrug, causing Sugar to give another snort of a laugh that made Kat upset enough to storm off. But really, her leaving was a win in my book; especially since it was timed almost perfectly with Selena finishing up her interviews.

As she headed our way, Sugar was quick to excuse herself, offering Selena a, *"Good job"* in passing that she graciously accepted before making her way over to me to address what I hadn't even realized she'd noticed. "Katianna didn't look very happy."

"She's not. But what's new?" I asked, rolling my eyes again as I thought back on her empty ass threat like it meant anything other than her just becoming even more annoying about this shit when we really didn't need her input at all.

Still, it was just like her to insert herself in anything she felt would affect her baby - *the Nymphs* - and have Selena concerned enough to ask, "Everything okay?"

Releasing a heavy sigh, I scrubbed a hand down my face and answered, "She just uh… *knows*. Walked up on Sugar and I talking about us."

Snapping her head back, Selena's eyes tightened when she hissed, "We agreed to keep it lowkey, and you told *Sugar* of all people? That's as good as sitting down with the local news!"

The same way she had defended me earlier, I was quick to stand up for Coach Daniels in her absence when I mentioned, "Actually, Sugar's known for a while and didn't say anything. She's apparently been hearin' us on the road, *after dark*."

"*Oh God…*" she groaned, bringing a grin to my lips as I told her, "Don't be all embarrassed now, lil' baby. If it's good to you, it's good to you."

"But my head coach knowing just how good it is to me is not exactly at the top of my list of things I need her to be informed on."

"So shut yo' ass up next time then," I suggested with a chuckle that made her smirk as she glanced at her phone for the time before changing the subject.

"I need to go to my room right quick. You comin'?"

As if she already knew what my answer would be,

she made a move out of the conference room towards the elevators, pushing the 'up' button to a glow as I finally replied, "A chance to have you all to myself? Hell yeah, I'm comin'."

Giggling, she insisted, "You can look, but I don't have time for touchin', big baby."

"Guess I gotta get all my touchin' in right now then," I teased the second we made it into the elevator, the fact that we were alone giving me the freedom to have my way as I pulled her back against me and started kissing on her neck from behind.

She was all moans and groans until she peeked up and noticed what was above us. "*Ooh.* Look at this mirror. Stand still so I can take a picture."

Keeping my same position with my arms wrapped around her waist and my face buried in the crook of her neck, Selena snapped a series of pictures using the reflection above us, the chime of the elevator signaling our arrival causing her to pull away from me just in case someone was waiting on her floor. And even though there was, she was still super vocal about expressing how pleased she was with the pictures she'd taken, scrolling through as she gushed, "These are *so* cute. I have to post at least one of 'em."

"*Selena…*" I groaned, knowing that probably wasn't the best idea as far as us staying lowkey went. But because her mind was already set on it, she didn't back down, using her free hand to pull her keycard from her pocket as she snapped, "*What?* I'm sick of having to play by everybody else's rules. And besides, you can't even really tell it's you. Just some tall, obviously fine ass man with a blur of tattoos on his arms."

To prove her point, she handed me her phone to

show me she wasn't lying. And while the picture did have a mystique about it, I still didn't think it was a good idea for her to post it.

This also wasn't a battle I really cared to win, though. And because of that, I was already preparing myself for the worst as I shook my head and told her, "Yeah, aight. If you say so."

It went viral.

I shouldn't have been all that surprised since of course everybody and they mama wanted to know who the mystery man was in the picture Selena Samuels had captioned, *"My Big Baby"* with the heart emoji. But because it had gone viral, I found myself in Las Vegas, *in late July*, wearing a jacket to cover my tattooed arms so people wouldn't be able to put two-and-two together so easily.

Of course it was inevitable that they'd find out about us eventually. But this was Selena's weekend, and I didn't want to cause any more of a stir than what that picture had already caused by making myself any easier to identify.

It helped that the casino arena where the Three-Point Shootout was being held was surely a lot cooler than the desert heat outside, giving me an excuse to keep my jacket on. But when I saw Kage Steele approaching me on my way over to the venue, I was ready to at least roll my sleeves up so I could whoop his ass, something he must've sensed since he immediately held his hands up to say, "Hear me out, fam. Just hear me out."

With that picture he'd posted on my mind, I didn't want to hear shit besides the impact of my fist clocking him in the jaw. But because we had a bit of an audience, I did my best to keep my composure and let him speak, opening and tightening my fist repeatedly to relieve some tension as I listened to what I hoped, *for his sake*, wouldn't be some weak ass explanation.

He started off on the right track when he blurted, "That shit I posted about you was foul. And for that, I apologize. I *just…* got caught up talkin' shit and drinkin' with my stupid ass friends that led to me doing some stupid ass shit with that shirt of your mugshot."

How drinking and talking shit turned into the production of a whole t-shirt, I wasn't sure. But I also knew these young niggas with money were resourceful as hell, leading me to address the more important part of his spiel when I told him, "I don't know why my name was in your mouth to begin with, but it sounds like you need better friends."

"You prolly right," he agreed with only half the enthusiasm I needed to hear.

I mean, I'd been there and done that. I'd lived what I thought was an invincible life and learned the hard way just how *vincible* I was. I'd had the friends who let me do all the dumb shit I wanted as long as it meant they'd be able to benefit from my lifestyle and knew how quickly that shit folded once the money stopped. And if I couldn't beat his ass like I wanted to, I was at least going to teach him a life lesson, getting right in his face to say, "Nah, ain't no probably. Better friends wouldn't be encouraging your ass to do childish shit like fuckin' with another man's livelihood for a little attention. They'd tell you to chill, protect your brand, and most importantly, protect your bag. I mean, you do realize that shit wasn't a good look on any level, right?"

Taking a step back to create some space between us, he held his hands up once again to express, "I hear you, fam. And again, I apologize; man to man."

On one hand, I still wanted to slap his young ass up. But on the other hand, it was his age that was saving him since I knew he still had a lot of maturing to do. And that was only proven even more so when, in the midst of all this, he found room to push past me so that he could introduce himself to the woman who had snuck up behind me.

He was all swag and slick talk when he extended his hand to say, "How you doin', baby? I'm Kage Steele, point guard for the Tennessee Trojans."

"Bleu Taylor, seasoned sports reporter who knows *all* about you," she replied with a friendly smile that really had Kage beaming.

"Oh yeah? Say more," he insisted, making her chuckle as she dropped her hand and replied, "*Or not.* I was just coming by to say hey to an old friend."

Redirecting her attention towards me, she was quick to tease, "I'm pretty sure this is the most I've seen you in years, Dre."

"Tell me about it," I sighed, accepting her quick hug as I told her, "The Nymphs are keepin' me busy."

"As they should be," she replied proudly. "But since your girl is also booked and busy, I need to get going. It was good seeing you, though. And it was nice to meet you, Kage."

"Likewise, Mrs. Taylor," he told her, using the oldest trick in the book to ask if she was married or not. And because I knew the answer, I was already shaking my head at what he was after, surprised to see Bleu play along when she made a point of tossing a correction over her shoulder.

"*Ms.* Taylor."

Watching her walk away, Kage let off a low whistle and groaned, "Now that's a bad bi…"

"Aye, man. Watch your mouth," I warned, finding it strange that he even felt comfortable saying some shit like that by me.

I mean, before today, he and I both knew he was on my *"on-sight"* list for that stunt he'd pulled online. But now that we were a little past that, he was already acting like we were homies, not holding anything back when he replied, "I'm sayin, though. Shorty is on another level. Sexy, grown, into sports, already knows the kid…"

Finding his confidence amusing, I chuckled and asked, "You really like aiming high, don't you?"

"What ol' MJ say? You miss a hundred percent of the shots you don't take?"

"That was actually a Wayne Gretzky quote," I corrected, Kage showing his age when he grumbled, "*Whoever that is…*"

Giving me a quick dap that, *again*, felt strange as hell considering the energy between us before today, he announced, "But aye. I'ma get to this Three-Point Shootout so I can watch our hometown girl get this trophy for being the greatest shooter to ever do it."

Even though his interest in the competition sounded legit, I couldn't help myself in scolding, "I know her shooting better be the only thing you're watchin'."

"So that was you in that picture she posted on IG, huh?" he realized, not even waiting for me to respond before he gave me another dap and complimented, "Respect, big homie. You won."

"Thanks?" I replied, more confused than anything as I watched him take-off towards a crowd of fans hoping to get a picture or his signature. But it was the uproar surrounding his arrival that gave me the opportunity to slip by without having to say much, finding Sugar in the section reserved for coaches where she'd saved me a seat.

Without much of a greeting, Sugar announced, "She's locked in, Dre. I think she's gonna win it."

"How sure are you? Cause this *is* Vegas, so you know you can bet on just about anything," I halfway joked, spotting Selena who was busy warming up on the court as Sugar backed up her claims.

"She has that look in her eyes. I know you know the one I'm talkin' about."

I *did* know what she was talking about. And because I knew what she was talking about, it wasn't all that surprising to me when Selena shot the first round like her life depended on it, easily making it to the finals where she was up against one of her old teammates from her LA days.

For her, the competition didn't really matter. It was all about *her* skill, *her* determination, *her* will to win the money for the charity of her choice and the trophy crowning her queen of the arc - *the three-point arc, that is.*

She didn't shy away from putting on a show though, the crowd on their feet as Selena approached the middle rack of balls after shooting a perfect percentage from the first two racks. And even there, she only missed the moneyball, the crowd giving a disappointed, *"Aww!"* since it messed up the opportunity for her to do the impossible by making it all the way around the arc without a miss.

Still, it was an impressive performance. And I felt proud as hell watching her last ball sink in, leaving her with a final score that almost doubled her opponent's who'd struggled under the pressure of the championship round.

Even while being celebrated by her peers from around the league, Selena somehow spotted me in the crowd to give me a smirk and a wink, something I thought was quick and innocent enough for no one to notice. But when Sugar shoulder-bumped me with a stupid grin on her face, I realized we'd have to be a lot more careful if we really expected to make it to the end of the season as a secret.

FIFTEEN

"I GOTTA BE HONEST, Selena. Las Vegas is growing on me a little bit."

My stare was filled with more disbelief than anything as I watched Ari tape my ankle in preparation for the All-Star Game later this afternoon, already sick that she was even considering the move since I wasn't sure what I'd do without her. I mean, sure any opportunity for growth in the field was a no-brainer, and the opening on the local team's training staff was very convenient. But still, I didn't want her to leave Nashville, frowning as I worked up my defense that sounded like a bunch of nonsense compared to the glitz and glamour of Vegas.

I had to try though, quick to ask, "But what about the Nymphs? I mean, you already get along so well with all of us. Here, you'd be starting all over with a bunch of women you might not even vibe with. And do you really wanna live in an annoying ass tourist city where people literally show up on their worst behavior? And think about your skin. It's so damn dry here, you'd probably turn into sandpaper."

Laughing, she replied, "Great con list, but I'm still gonna consider it. I mean, don't get me wrong, I love Nashville. But it's also like Nashville down here and Las Vegas up here as far as overall city rankings go."

Glancing at the difference between the heights she'd created with her hands, I commented, "Don't do my hometown. It's not that low."

"But it's *your* hometown, so of course you have some special ties," she argued like I wouldn't have a defense for that too.

"I lived out in LA and still had my reasons to come home."

"Yeah. *A job*," she emphasized with another chuckle. "Which was the same thing that brought me to Nashville and the same thing that could bring me out here to Las Vegas if I so choose."

Because there wasn't much more I could say about it without sounding whiny and ridiculous, I ended on my personal truth. "I still think Nashville is the better choice."

"I bet you do; especially now that you're all boo'd up and barely have time to go out for drinks with your main bitch," she joked, holding up her hands to add, "*Not that I'm hatin'*. Cause trust and believe, I'd diss your ass for Dre Leonard too."

Peeking around at the other folks in the training room who weren't really paying us any mind, I still whispered, "Will you keep it down?"

"You're right. That picture you posted was loud enough," she replied with a chuckle that made me roll my eyes before offering an explanation.

"It was an act of defiance."

"Which I support cause it was also cute as shit," Ari mentioned, something I had to agree with since Dre and I had always been cute together long before we were even a thing.

Just the thought of how far we'd come had me grinning as I slipped my shoe back on so that I could hop down from the training table, resting my hand on Ari's shoulder as I groaned, "*Anyway*. Thanks for getting me together. And don't get too comfortable in here."

"Mmhm, we'll see," she replied with a smirk before sending me to join the rest of my team for the weekend out on the court for warmups. But when I saw who was already making himself cozy in his courtside seats, I made a detour, my eyes squinted as I observed his attire that looked a little *too* familiar.

Once he saw me heading his way, he cheered, "*Dun-a-dun-a-dun-a-dun-a-dun* The Champ is here!" making me shake my head as I addressed what really had my attention.

"Kage, where the hell did you get this jersey?"

It was a replica of the one I'd worn back at Lynstone, essentially a Selena Samuels exclusive that he only had me even more curious about when he answered, "I have my ways." And before I could ask for more information, he put a hand to my arm to say, "Congratulations on that monster performance last night."

"I appreciate it," I replied with a nod, crossing my arms over my chest as I continued, "But I also have a bone to pick with you. Cause that shirt of Dre you posted was…"

Before I could even finish, he raised his hand to cut

me off. "I've already apologized to him. But I suppose I should apologize to you too, seeing that that's your man now."

Frowning, I asked, "Who told you that?" wondering if my act of defiance might've really been as loud as Ari had insisted.

But when Kage answered, "He did," I only grew more confused. And I suppose it was that confusion that prompted him to explain, "I mean, not *directly*. But he was just about ready to knock me out for even mentioning you, and I respect it cause I'd be ready to knock a nigga out over your pretty ass too."

"Don't get too ahead of yourself, K," I warned, knowing Dre was still close enough to follow through on that if he got too fresh with me.

Thankfully, he changed the subject, clapping his hands together when he said, "*Aye*. But on some real shit, I need you reppin' for the set somethin' heavy during this game today cause I've been talkin' mad shit to the other niggas that are here from the league about our sister squad being the best."

"*Oh my God, Kage…*" I sighed with an amused giggle, shaking my head at the fact that his loyalty to everything Nashville already ran so deep.

That amusement only grew when he asked, "Am I lying? You can tell me if I'm lying."

"Our record indicates you're telling the truth. And the only reason I'm here is to, *as you put it*, rep for the set somethin' heavy," I answered, putting him somewhat at ease according to his response.

"That's what I like to hear then. Now lemme go give my suga' mama Sugar the same pep talk."

"*Boy…*" I groaned, giggling again as I watched him

do a little jog towards where Sugar was standing on the sidelines watching our team warm-up. And with his exit came Dre's arrival, his innocent hand resting at the top of my back when he asked, "You good, lil' baby?"

I did him one better when I turned his way with a smile and answered, "Actually, I'm great."

You would've thought I'd said something crazy the way Dre's eyebrows furrowed in response, a look of concern on his face once he acknowledged, "You seem *very*... relaxed."

Giggling, I reminded him, "It's an All-Star Game, Dre. It's supposed to be relaxed, right?"

"Yeah, but I also know you. And for you, basketball is typically a *very* serious thing."

Shaking my head, I told him, "Not today. Today, I'm having fun with it."

It sounded good coming off my lips. But as soon as the game started, I realized that wouldn't be the case at all, the other team on some hyper-competitive shit from the very beginning that forced me and my squad to rise to the occasion. And we did for the most part, the game going down to the wire but ending in a loss that had me annoyed since I hadn't come all the way to Las Vegas to lose.

At least I had my Three-Point Shootout trophy to give some sort of balance, still feeling a way about the whole thing when I received a text from Dre to meet him in his suite. And while I pouted the entire walk there, I couldn't help but smile after he opened the door and pulled me inside before demanding that I get naked.

"You really think I'm that easy? Cause for you, I totally am," I told him playfully, already getting rid of the *Nike* slides, sweatpants, and hoodie I'd thrown on after the game as he laughed me off.

"If I only wanted to fuck, I would've just come down to your room," he replied, pulling me deeper into his suite towards his bed that was surrounded by candles and covered in rose petals with an assortment of oils sitting on the nightstand nearby.

"Dre, what's all this?" I asked, already finding his efforts adorably romantic before he even gave an explanation.

"I know how you get after a loss. So I thought a massage might make you feel a little better."

Now I was even more impressed, turning his way to ask, "You went and got all of this after the game?"

Nodding, he chuckled and replied, "You'd be surprised how easy it is to get this exact assortment of items out here in Vegas."

"*Now that you mention it…*" I muttered, joining in on his chuckle as he urged, "Go lay down, lil' baby. Let me get you right."

He didn't have to tell me twice, my bra and panties the last things to go as I laid face down on his mattress. And it wasn't long after that Dre was beginning the massage I already knew I'd be thanking him for later with as much pussy as he wanted, his hands feeling heavenly as he worked my shoulders and asked, "Pressure okay?"

"Perfect," I piped out, slobbering a little on the pillow tucked under my head by the time he made it down to my lower back. And when he got to my ass and thighs, I was just waiting for him to slip a finger into either hole, frowning a little when he very politely continued down to my calves.

It was worth it though, particularly when he got down to my feet that he took his time with like he just knew they needed the extra attention. Either that, or he was just really enjoying himself, seeming like the latter when he commented, "I could do this all night."

"If you're asking for permission, the answer is hell yes," I moaned, making him chuckle as he spread my legs and slowly started making his way back up my body.

"Nah, I have somethin' better in mind. Somethin' you might enjoy even more."

Because what he was doing already felt so damn good, I didn't want to risk exchanging it for anything less exhilarating, quick to tell him, "If the chances are only *"might"*, you can just keep doing what you're doing."

"You mean, you don't want me to do this instead?" he asked, running a finger against my slick folds that made me gasp and made him groan, "*Mmm.* What's that all about?"

"You touching me, that's what."

I expected him to go in for more, but he didn't, only building the anticipation when he popped me on the ass and urged, "Turn over. I'm not done."

While laying on my stomach allowed me at least a little bit of coverage, laying on my back left me wide open, my eyes low as I watched Dre pour more oil onto his hands. And after rubbing them together to get the oil to a more pleasing temperature, he hovered over me and started rubbing behind my ears down to my collarbone, being able to see him only making the whole thing even sexier; only making me even wetter.

Crazy enough, that wasn't the only thing that had

turned me on about Dre today, my voice a little groggy when I mentioned, "Kage told me you two talked."

"Definitely not tryna talk about Kage right now," he replied with a humorless laugh, making me realize I hadn't even really scratched the surface of why I'd brought him up.

So without wasting any more time, I explained, "He told me he apologized. He also told me you were just about ready to whoop his ass over me. That's kinda hot, Dre."

I expected that to help him understand. But according to the irritated look on his face, it had only made things worse, his lips turned into a frown when he asked, "Me acting up and possibly getting in real trouble for it during a weekend all about you and your league is hot?"

Shaking my head, I reasoned, "Not in that context. But like, the idea of you choking somebody out…"

"Like this?" he asked with a smirk, cutting me off with a firm hand around my neck that sent the rest of my body into a frenzy.

Not because I thought he'd choke me out for real. But because it was so damn sexy, and I wished it was paired with his dick deep inside of me.

Unfortunately, I was the only one naked enough for that to even be possible. But when he asked, "Are you gonna let me finish?" I took that as an opportunity to get him on my level, licking my lips to bargain, "Only if you take your clothes off to do it."

Like it was nothing, Dre made quickwork of climbing from the bed to pull off both his shirt and pants, getting ready to leave his briefs on until I raised an eyebrow and demanded, "Those too."

Smirking, he ditched his briefs to show off the erection I mentally took credit for before returning to the bed. And while I fully expected him to give in now that we were both undressed, he held strong, his dick propped up against my leg as he added a little more oil to his hands then took his time massaging my breasts to the point that I started to beg for him to be done.

"Greedy, greedy, greedy," he teased, continuing to taunt me by giving my quads some attention they really didn't need. And I was just about ready to either implement some sort of reverse psychology strategy or straight up attack his ass when he draped one of my legs over his shoulder so that we were finally aligned, only building more anticipation as he ran the tip of his dick against my clit and teased, "Aww man. I forget to do your arms."

"Dre, if you don't…"

The rest of my words transformed into a moan as he plunged into me, going as deep as my body would allow him to before pulling out to do it again. And this time, he reached new depth, the wetness in combination with how relaxed my body was thanks to the massage creating a symphony of pleasure that made Dre grunt, "Nah, this shit feels *too* fuckin' good."

He was right.

It *did* feel too fuckin' good. And I was enthusiastic about letting him know that with every stroke, gripping into his back, and his shoulders, and his ass, and basically anything I could get my hands on while he continued to imprint himself on my inner walls. But when he slowed it down and paired his careful strokes with deep tongue kisses, I assumed he was trying to imprint himself on my entire being, my toes curling as he sexed me with unspoken feelings like this was about much more than just making me feel better about the game.

Nah, Dre was trying to tell me something.

Exactly what that was, I wasn't sure. But because of the way our souls had tied in such a short period of time, I felt it in my gut, I felt it in my heart, I just... *felt it.* And I felt *him*, using intimacy to pour into me in ways he'd never done before.

It was intense, and a little overwhelming. But it also felt so good that I didn't want him to stop, tears reaching my ducts as my nerves were flooded with the static of my approaching orgasm. And with his special knowledge of my body, Dre did exactly what he had to do to send me over the moon, sexing me through it to get his own that he just barely pulled out of me in time to release all over my clit.

He was still grunting with aftershocks when I teased, "Looks like your pull-out game needs a little work."

"Practice makes perfect, right?" he fired back with the sexiest smirk, planting a kiss on my cheek before leaving the bed to go clean himself up. And while I planned to follow him to the bathroom so I could do the same, the heavy desire for a quick catnap came first, feeling grateful that Dre knew to return with a warm towel so that he could wipe up his mess and kiss me goodnight.

SIXTEEN

WITH ONLY FIFTEEN games following All-Star week-end, it felt like the season was flying by. And honestly, with how well everything was finally going in my world, I wished it would slow the hell down. I mean, the Nymphs were thriving, my relationship with Selena was blossoming on a daily, I'd successfully finished my online course. Even my mother was making good progress in her rehabilitation program, calling every so often to check-in which was something we'd never done.

It was nice, though.

Different, but appreciated since it kept me from worrying about her even if the worrying was mostly subconscious. And not only that, but it allowed me to focus even more on my own shit, my emotional tank full enough to really experience everything that came with falling in love with Selena Samuels.

Yeah, that shit was happening whether I wanted it to or not. But she made it so damn easy and fun that I would've been a fool not to welcome the feeling with open arms, a smile on my face as I watched her warm up for our home game against Seattle.

They were the top team in the Western Conference, making tonight's game something like a tone-setter for the playoffs coming up. And even though the only way we'd actually play against them was if - *when* - we both advanced to the finals, it was still important that we let them know they didn't want no smoke with us in a best-of-five situation.

We were coming for it all.

Before I'd accepted the job, I honestly wasn't sure how easy that "we" would come, wasn't sure if it would ever feel quite natural, didn't know if I'd ever feel apart. But over the course of the season, I'd not only grown to respect how hard these women worked and the high level at which they competed, but I'd also grown connected to the other coaches and players as people, feeling like I'd gained a gang of sisters who I'd ride for in a heartbeat.

Well... all except for one; that one deserving of much more than just familial loyalty. And with every day that passed, I did my best to show her that, letting my actions speak for me in ways words wouldn't do any justice.

She felt it though. And not only did she feel it, she knew just how to reciprocate it.

Even now as I sat on the bench at the opposite end of the court, she found a moment to peek over her shoulder to shoot me a smile, turning back around just as quickly to catch a pass from one of the trainers who was walking her through her pregame drills. And considering how laser-focused she was maneuvering through those, I knew we were in for an entertaining game, feeling excited about it as a heavy presence filled the seat next to mine.

There were only a handful of people I held in high regard and the person with the presence easily sat at the top of the list, his energy speaking for him long before he even said a word. And when he did, I was completely tuned in, ready to receive whatever message he came to deliver that turned out to be much simpler than I expected.

"I'm proud of you, Dre."

Coming from Mr. Philip Lloyd - patriarch of the Lloyd family who owned the Tennessee Trojans and the man who, *with his daughter Katianna*, had taken a chance on me - those words felt like the ultimate gold star, a grin on my lips as I turned his way to say, "I appreciate that, sir."

Nodding, he continued, "A lot of men in your position would've frowned down on an opportunity like this, thinking they were too good for the WNBA. But you? You've taken it and ran with it. You've made this assistant coaching position your own. And that not only speaks to your character, but also your knowledge of the game since this is clearly panning out to be a special season for the Nymphs."

I couldn't have agreed more with his sentiment about this season feeling special, giving praise where it was due when I replied, "I wish I could take credit, but Katianna assembled a very talented squad."

With a wave of his hand, he teased, "Ah, I'll let you brag on your girl Selena later," catching me off-guard since I didn't even know he knew about that. Then again, with Katianna being his daughter, I shouldn't have been surprised that she'd tattled on us; though it didn't seem like Mr. Lloyd cared either way as he continued, "Anyway. I was hoping we could make some time to discuss your future with the Trojans."

"You mean the Nymphs?"

Shaking his head, he put a heavy hand to my shoulder to reply, "I said it right the first time, Dre." And he must've noticed the confusion on my face since he knew to explain, "Putting you with the Nymphs was really more of a test to see how serious you were about coaching, to see how committed you'd be as the season went on, *to...* really make sure you were taking better care of yourself. And now that that's proven, I have a spot on the Trojans staff with your name on it."

"Wow. *I...* I don't know what to say."

"A smart man would say yes based off the pay raise alone," he suggested with a chuckle. "But I understand if the decision is a little more complicated than that now."

As if to put extra meaning behind his words, he gave a little nod towards the court where Selena was just finishing up her drills, dabbing at the sweat she'd worked up with the hem of her warm-up shirt before moving to sign a few pregame autographs for the fans who had arrived extra early. And after granting a few pictures too, she made her way over to us, skipping past me to greet Mr. Lloyd with an extremely casual, "Hey Phil."

No one I knew had ever gotten away with calling him Phil, something he was typically firm about with anyone he came across. But of course Selena had special privileges that had Mr. Lloyd standing up from his chair to give her both a shoulder hug and a cheek kiss before asking, "You're gonna put those pacific northwesterners to shame tonight, right?"

"Wouldn't have shown up today if that wasn't in the plans," she replied sharply, her grin from earlier replaced with a scowl that told us both she was very serious about what she'd just said.

Mr. Lloyd was digging the energy, acknowledging so when he wagged his finger and commented, "*See*. I need someone like you on the Trojans. Like that one movie, *Juwanna Mann*, but the other way around."

The idea made me chuckle. But because Selena was already in the zone, she hardly even flinched as she told him, "You have plenty me's, Phil. Just gotta have the right coach to know what to do with them."

With a raised eyebrow, Mr. Lloyd challenged, "Are you saying Coach Kirkwood doesn't have the juice?"

"I'm sayin' Niko, Kage, and Zeb are way too solid of a core for the Trojans to have lost in the playoffs even if no one really expected them to be there in the first place. But hey, what do I know?" she told him with a passive-aggressive smirk, excusing herself to head to the locker room and leaving Mr. Lloyd with something to think about according to the inquisitive look on his face.

He didn't speak on it though, instead choosing to comment, "I can tell you have your hands full with that one, young man."

"In the best way possible," I told him with a proud smile, happy to have my hands overflowing with everything Selena. And when I finally joined her in the locker room for Sugar's pregame rundown, I couldn't stop myself from watching her even though she was paying me no mind, completely tuned into what Coach was saying before Mikayla took over to hype everyone up in a way only she could.

By the time she was finished, I was convinced the squad would've ran through the wall if the locker room door wasn't already opened for them. *Well...* everyone except for Selena who stayed back so that we could share what had become something like our pregame ritual - a special handshake with way too many parts and two quick kisses; one to her forehead and the second on her lips.

Other than general basketball stuff, that was often the only real communication we'd have before any game since Selena was a stickler about her routine. And tonight was no different, Selena jogging to catch up to her teammates before they entered the court to a chorus of much-deserved cheers from the crowd.

It was honestly fascinating to see just how much support they had, especially when compared to some of the other teams around the league who often struggled to fill up even the smallest of arenas to no fault of their own. But here, things were different. The fandom was dynamic, the energy was electric. And when The Golden Geras - *the senior citizen dance team that the Nymphs and Trojans shared* - came out to perform before tip-off, it only turned the knob up on the electricity that was already fueling the crowd which, in turn, fueled our squad who jumped out to an early twelve to two lead with Selena scoring six of the twelve.

Yeah, lil' baby was in her bag tonight. And I couldn't have been prouder as I watched her do exactly what she'd planned to do in putting the pacific northwest-erners to shame, splashing back-to-back shots from three-point land that brought her personal point total to twelve in less than four minutes and forced Seattle to call a timeout so they could regroup.

That only fired Selena up even more, pounding her chest as her teammates crowded around her with hi-fives and shoulder bumps that I enjoyed from a distance since getting too close to her in a moment like this would've only been a distraction. But when I saw Selena staring out into the crowd with a rare mid-game grin compared to her typical stoic look, I couldn't help following her line of vision, quickly realizing the reason for her turn-up was beyond just setting the tone for the playoffs.

Mr. Samuels was there. And not only was he there, he was wiping tears from his eyes and pointing to the ceiling while Selena gnawed on her lip like she was holding back her own emotions as she rubbed the heart tattoo dedicated to her mother and brother on the back of her shoulder.

It was a special moment even if no one else caught it. And I made a mental note to ask her about it later, the buzzer signaling the end of the timeout locking her right back in for the rest of the first quarter that got a little more competitive. Still, the Nymphs remained in control of the tempo, maintaining the lead into halftime that only gave them more confidence going into the second half. But Seattle wasn't going down without a fight, stunning the crowd to silence when they tied the game in the third quarter and reminded everyone why they were the top team in the West.

Since her quick start, Selena had gone a little cold from behind the arc, only adding a few free throws and a lay-up to her point total for the game. But on defense, she'd turned into a pest, putting all of her energy into getting much-needed stops that allowed our offense to flourish with easy fastbreak points and gave us a comfortable lead going into the final minutes of the game.

Because we didn't want to run the risk of anyone getting hurt with the playoffs on the horizon, we took the starters out one by one, including Selena who received a standing ovation for her efforts in leading the charge. But as she made her way down the bench giving hi-fives to the rest of the team, I couldn't help noticing how winded she seemed; something that was unusual for her, especially at this point in the season when she should've been in her best physical shape.

"You good, lil' baby?" I asked once she plopped down in the seat next to mine on the bench, watching her chest heave as she leaned against the back of the chair as if to open herself up to receive more air.

"I'm fine," she breathed heavily before taking a long drag from the water bottle one of the trainers had given her, still blowing hard out of her nose after she swallowed it down.

Skeptically, I pressed, "You sure? You seem a little gassed."

"I said I'm fine," she repeated with a bit of an attitude that told me something was up. But because the game wasn't quite over yet, I didn't push her on it, waiting for the final buzzer to sound so we could shake hands with the other team.

Of course, that was only the beginning of Selena's postgame obligations. There was the courtside interview, the time spent signing more autographs, the motivational speech from Sugar in the locker room, the press conference. And because she had family in attendance, she had to spend a little time with them too before finally making her way back around to me.

Not that I was complaining.

It was just the reality of being with someone in high demand, though I seemed to be the only one to notice the smile on her lips wasn't quite meeting her eyes. And once we were alone, I wasted no time getting to the bottom of it, my eyebrow piqued when I asked, "What's up with you, SeSa?"

I figured using her nickname would cue her in on the fact that my concern was legit. But for whatever reason, she still got a little defensive anyway, frowning as she questioned, "What are you talkin' about, Dre?"

"Your energy. Something seems... *I don't know*. Off," I explained, watching her body language closely to see if it would tell me what I had a feeling her mouth wouldn't.

She played it cool though, only shrugging as she reasoned, "That game took a lot out of me."

"Because your father was there?"

"No, because I played hard," she defended, something I agreed with even though I knew there had to be more to the story since her playing hard wasn't anything new.

"I'll give you that. But I've also never seen you so exhausted."

With a chuckle, she groaned, "*Damn*. A girl can't get a little winded every once in a while? Those Seattle girls were quick, and I'm not exactly getting any younger."

"You're not even five years outta college, Selena," I reminded her with a little chuckle of my own, catching her smirk before she offered a rebuttal.

"But I also play year-round which means I'm essentially putting double the miles on my body. I think that shit is starting to catch up with me."

Even though I was still feeling a little skeptical, her explanation made reasonable enough sense for me to reply, "Well at least you'll get a little bit of extra time off to rest with these first and second-round byes in the playoffs."

It was a unique format that the *WNBA* followed with the top two teams getting a ticket straight to the semi-finals instead of having to play in each round, giving us a bit of an advantage that Selena was already relishing in when she replied, "And I'll need every bit of it, including one of those special massages you give. You know, the one that comes with the side of dick."

Wrapping her in a hug, I told her, "We can make that happen, as long as you assure me you're really as fine as you're claiming to be."

"Don't I look it?" she asked playfully, making me roll my eyes as I groaned, *"You know what I mean."*

Pressing her hands into my chest, she pleaded, "I'm fine, Dre. *Really.* Just extra tired. But I'm good."

"You sure?"

"Positive," she nodded. "Now let's get outta here before I have to bust your ass on the court again."

Shaking my head, I kept my arm wrapped around her shoulder as I teased, "Nah, you ain't got the range today, lil' baby. I need it to be fair and square when I run you off the court."

"That'll never happen, but I appreciate your... *mmph.*"

The pained expression on her face that followed her grunt made my concern from earlier return, watching as she held her side and groaned, "It's just a little cramp," before moving from under my arm so that she could stretch it out. But as she continued to wince through the pain even after it became a bit more tolerable, I knew one thing was for certain.

My news about the job offer with the Trojans was going on the backburner until I figured out what was really going on with her.

SEVENTEEN

SOMETHING WASN'T RIGHT.

I'd had my extra time off to rest. I felt fine going through my normal, pregame routine. I'd even played less minutes tonight thanks to our first playoff game turning into a blowout victory. But as I sat in the locker room listening to Sugar's postgame speech about this win only being the beginning, I still felt tired as hell like I'd played every minute of a game that had gone into triple overtime, my heart pounding like it hadn't been in a resting state for at least a half hour now.

Maybe my nerves just hadn't settled yet.

There was something about high stakes games that always made me more anxious than normal, even going back to my days of playing AAU ball as a teenager. But I had never experienced anxiety to the point of nausea, literally gagging when I caught a whiff of Mikayla's shoes the second she removed them.

"Gotdamn, Mik. I know those rookie checks aren't much, but I'm sure you can afford to replace those stinky ass sneakers," I whispered, covering my nose as

Mikayla picked them up to take a sniff for herself. And I was surprised that she didn't pass out because of it, only frowning as she brushed me off to catch the end of Sugar's speech that encouraged us to rest up before our next game in less than forty-eight hours.

Not like I had a choice.

I needed all the recovery time I could get, hoping that would be enough for the nerves to pass so that I could really lock in for game two. But when it finally rolled around, it was practically a repeat performance for the anxiety-inducing exhaustion that had me wheezing hard enough to draw concern from Ari who suggested we go see the team doctor once the game was over and won.

Since there was no way in hell I was running the risk of missing the rest of the playoffs because of whatever the doctor found, I did my best to assure her I was fine. But my obvious fatigue said otherwise, a frown on Ari's face when she asked, "You're not coming down with somethin', are you?"

I shook my head no.

"Heart problems run in your family? Have you ever had a panic attack?"

Again, I shook my head no.

"Are you pregnant?"

Snapping my head back, I repeated, "*Pregnant?* Girl, bye," laughing her off as I waited for her to offer up more possibilities. But when she only raised an eyebrow in response, I gave it a second thought, realizing it wasn't all that impossible since Dre and I hadn't exactly been playing it the safest as of late.

Not since, *well*, before Las Vegas when we'd explored new territory and never felt the need to go back to using condoms on a consistent basis. But now, even without knowing for sure what was happening, I wished we would've just so I wouldn't have had to deal with the lingering uncertainty that had Ari putting a supportive hand to my knee to suggest, "Maybe you should take a pregnancy test. Just to know for sure."

The truth was, I didn't want to know for sure because I didn't want it to be a possibility at all, already feeling emotional about it when I sighed, "Ari, I can't be pregnant. Not right now."

There was still so much work to be done, so much basketball to be played; not only for the Nymphs but for my overseas team as well. And even beyond that, what would a baby mean for Dre and I who were still relatively new as a couple? How could I have a coach for a baby daddy when I still hadn't even been able to open up about him being my damn boyfriend?

I appreciated Ari's optimism when she insisted, "Well the earlier you know for sure, the better. Because if it's not that, it could be something even more serious."

"What's more serious than a whole ass baby?!" I whined, Ari chuckling a little bit in response even though there wasn't a damn thing funny.

"Okay, maybe not *more* serious. But there could still be something going on with your health that needs to be addressed, babe."

Only because of that was I willing to take the test. But not until after we'd already won game three, sweeping the series and securing our spot in the finals. And thankfully, LA and Seattle were still battling it out on the other side of the bracket, giving us another small break and giving me a little more time to process the possibility of a baby.

A baby.

With my career being so physically demanding year-round, I hadn't really had the chance to give motherhood much thought. And not only that, but I'd also never been with someone even worth sharing that kind of life-changing experience with, quickly coming to the conclusion that I must've really loved me some Jordan DeAndre Leonard since his involvement was the only bright spot in all of this even if I couldn't tell him about it just yet.

He was already worried enough for reasons I hadn't understood. But after finally taking the test in Ari's bathroom, I realized his concern was valid, tears welling up in my eyes as I stared down at the two pink lines that would change everything.

With a knock on the door that broke my gaze, Ari called out, "You okay in there, babe?" my blink in response causing a tear to hit my cheek as I stood up to let her in. And with one look at my face, she already knew the answer to her question.

No.

I wasn't okay.

"Aww, Selena," she sighed, pulling me into a hug that made me burst into tears as I cried, "How could I have let this happen?!"

Rubbing soft circles on my back, Ari did her best to calm me down as she assured, "Selena, you're gonna be okay. We'll figure it out. You have options."

Honestly, I couldn't even think that far ahead yet, stuck on the fact that this wasn't exactly something I could just keep to myself. And because I was unsure of what his reaction would be since this was totally unplanned, I found myself crying even harder when I asked, "But how am I gonna tell Dre?"

"The same way you'd tell him anything," she replied simply, though I knew it was a little more complicated than that.

"I can't. He's already been so concerned about my health lately. This will just make him *insufferable*."

"So don't tell him until after the finals," Ari suggested as she guided me over to her bed to sit down, surely tired of having to hold up my weight since I'd been using her for support ever since I broke the news.

But even when we were seated, I rested my head on her shoulder, sniffling as I reasoned, "But he needs to know. We have *to*... make a decision."

If there was one thing I'd learned about being a professional athlete as a woman, it was that there was no right time to get pregnant. No matter what, it was treated as an inconvenience, a defect, a *weakness*; like pregnancy and giving birth was just some easy thing to do.

Still, with that came a very personal decision to make in terms of whether or not to terminate while it was still early enough to do so, something plenty of women in my position had done in order to continue competing. And for that reason, I was glad to have Ari on my side who was completely supportive when she grabbed my hands to say, "Selena, just tell me what you need, and we'll make it happen."

Gnawing on my lip, I pushed out, "What I need, is a doctor's appointment."

She was already grabbing her phone to make arrangements when she replied, "You know the team doctor is always on call. I can..."

"*No*," I cut her off. "I need something more private than that. Cause the team doctor is way too close to Katianna, and that's the last person I need finding out right now."

I could only imagine how livid she'd be when she learned I was pregnant, finding some way to make it about her and the Nymphs instead of considering my well-being. And since the absolute last thing I needed was additional stress on top of what I was already experiencing, I was grateful when Ari didn't fight me on it, only giving a nod as she replied, "Let me make a few calls and see what I can do."

Six weeks.

That's how far along I was according to the OB/GYN's calculations, proving our disregard for safe sex post-All-Star weekend had indeed been the cause of this beautiful nightmare.

Beautiful because I knew he or she was made with love even if Dre and I hadn't shared those exact words yet. And a nightmare because there were literally only three wins standing between me and the championship, and this baby was already sucking the life out of me.

At least it was still early enough in the pregnancy for me to be cleared to play.

That was my main concern, having everything I'd worked so hard for literally be snatched away from me in the blink of an eye. But even in the midst of a crisis, God had done me the biggest favor by keeping my body in good enough shape to still be able to compete in what was easily going to be the most important games of my life even though I had no idea what would come afterwards.

I mean, keeping the baby meant my overseas season was for sure a wash, not only cutting into the growth of my international brand but also my bankroll in a major way since the salary I made playing over there was a huge chunk of my income. And even beyond that, it wasn't a guarantee that I'd have a healthy pregnancy, or a healthy delivery, *or* be ready to come back to basketball right after giving birth when next season rolled around.

The shit *just*… wasn't fair on so many levels.

Being with child should've been a beautiful discovery worth celebrating, a happy time in my life. But because of my career, the only thing I could see it for was the potential professional disaster and that was before I'd even gotten the chance to tell the person who'd gone half on it.

I couldn't tell him.

Not yet.

Not until I'd finished the job in bringing a championship to Nashville.

I couldn't carry the weight of Dre's concern *and* the weight of having the team on my shoulders. I couldn't let this pregnancy completely distract me from the goal that was already within my reach. I couldn't *just*… give up.

I was fine, the baby was fine, and we were going to get this title together.

That's what I had settled on by the time Ari asked, "So what are you gonna do, Selena?"

Without letting a moment pass, I answered, "I'm gonna win."

To anyone else, it might've sounded like the wrong

response. But Ari knew exactly what I meant, giving an enthusiastic nod as she wrapped her arm around my shoulder and sang, "That's my girl."

Her continued support made a tear fall, but I was quick to wipe it away when she asked, "You know there's no way I can leave Nashville now, right? Not until I meet my niece or nephew."

Snapping my head back, I challenged, "Oh, so you'll stay for the baby, but not for me? You ain't real."

"My fake ass got a private doctor to see you in a moment's notice though," she defended, making me giggle as I nodded to agree.

"You did. And I love you for life for doing so," I told her, resting my head against the side of hers with an easy smile until I felt my phone vibrate with a text we read together.

"Where you at, lil' baby? I miss you." - Jordan

"*Hold up.* Who the hell is Jordan?" Ari asked with a frown as I sat up to send a response, already chuckling about her confusion as I typed and answered her question simultaneously.

"Jordan DeAndre Leonard is my baby daddy," I told her before pressing send.

"About to be on my way home. Miss you more." - SeSa

Our extra days off before the finals couldn't have been timed more perfectly for Dre since they'd finally found a buyer for his grandmother's house, sending him to St. Louis on a flight I had to force him to take because driving would've taken far too long. And I assumed him texting me to see where I was meant he was back from his trip and wanted to see me, though I wasn't sure if I was quite ready to face him alone.

Maybe I could get Ari to come too.

Of course she was still stuck on the random fun fact I had dropped, a bit hysterical when she squealed, "That nigga's name is Jordan?! Since when?"

Giggling, I answered, "Since birth. It's a long story. You should have him tell it when you come over for dinner tonight."

"You're not asking me to come over so I can be a buffer for when you drop the baby bomb, are you?" she asked skeptically, only making me giggle more as I shook my head while rubbing my still very flat tummy.

"No, Ari. The baby will not be a topic for discussion tonight."

"And you're not cooking, right? Cause whatever you made the last time you cooked for us had me beatboxing with my ass."

"Ari!" I squealed as I bust out laughing, falling into her as she laughed along with me and defended, "I'm just sayin', girl. God gave you a lot of talents, but cooking did *not* make the cut. Not by a long shot."

Rolling my eyes, I groaned, "*Anyway.* You comin'? We can order from whatever takeout place you want, except for the places you know I don't like cause that just wouldn't be fair."

"You really think I'd do my Godbaby like that?" she

teased with a hand to my stomach, somehow making it a little realer than when I'd done it myself. And even though the whole thing still had me completely shook, I was beyond grateful to be in good company, giving me a bit of calm before what was sure to be one hell of a storm.

EIGHTEEN

OUR SECRET WAS on the verge of collapsing.

It was the morning of the first game of the finals. And instead of people talking about what was sure to be the series of the decade between the Nymphs and Seattle - *a team that was only in its second season vs. a team on the verge of being back-to-back champions* - all of the attention was on Selena and I thanks to some eager ass social media intern from *Spilling That Hot Tea* who'd published a post linking the two of us as a couple.

There were the pictures we'd taken together during media day at the very beginning of the season along with a screenshot of the "relationship name" poll that Mikayla must've posted on her *Instagram* story around the same time. There was some old ass picture of Selena and I walking through the airport with her arm wrapped around mine and a picture one of her relatives must've posted of the two of us laughing about some-thing at her father's cookout. And finally, there was a zoomed-in version of the picture Selena had posted of us in the elevator side-by-side with a closeup picture of the tattoos on my arms. All clues that weren't exactly clear-cut evidence, but still plenty to keep the conversation alive and have my line pinging with calls from Katianna that I couldn't answer until I checked on Selena.

Of course, because of how early it was, she was still half-sleep when she answered my *FaceTime* call and groaned, "Something better be on fire, Jordan."

"*Eh...* something like that. And since you're just waking up, I'm assuming you don't know what it is," I replied, watching as she sat up in bed and started to stretch; lowkey distracting me from what I was calling her about since she always looked so damn pretty in the morning with her fresh skin, a scarf tied around her head, and those perfect braless titties.

In fact, I was just getting ready to comment on them when she finally responded, "Humor me."

Instead of explaining anything, I told her, "Check your *Instagram*."

"*Can't.* I let Ari change the passwords to all of my social media accounts so that I wouldn't have any distractions," she replied, squinting at the top of her screen when she muttered, *"Why is Kat texting me right now?"*

Because I had a feeling Katianna was on some other shit, I was quick to suggest, "*Don't...* read those yet. It'll sound better comin' from me."

"What will sound better coming from you?" she asked, confused until I went on to tell her about everything that had been posted about us online.

With the timing of it all, I expected Selena to freak out a little bit - *a lot of bit.* But she didn't, only waving me off as she sighed, "Oh, Dre. That's the least of my concerns right now."

"Seriously?"

"Yes, seriously," she nodded. "I could hardly sleep last night thinking about... tonight's game. I don't think I even have the capacity to worry about stupid people on the internet too."

It was the right approach, *the smart approach*, choosing to stay focused on the finals instead of letting any of that nonsense get into her head. And because she wasn't in a mood about it, I felt comfortable teasing, "Should've let me stay the night. I would've put your ass *right* to sleep."

Giggling, she reminded me, "No distractions, big baby. Not even from your fine ass."

"You're the fine one. Over there glowing and shit like your breath don't stink," I joked, making her laugh again as she hissed, *"Shut up,"* before putting me on pause to check the texts from our boss.

"Oh, this actually isn't as bad as I thought it would be."

"What'd she say?" I asked before admitting, "I ain't even answer her calls."

"Scaredy cat," Selena mumbled with another giggle, then read the texts out loud.

"Don't answer to anything." - KL

"Don't admit anything." - KL

"No comment. Redirect. No comment." - KL

"Sounds easy enough," I told her, finding it similar to the media training I'd done with Kat before the season had even started.

Selena didn't seem as enthused about it though, glancing down as she grumbled, "Yeah. Easy for now."

"*For now?*"

Instead of answering my question, she pulled the camera closer to her face to say, "I need to get up and start my day. See you at the arena in a few hours?"

Frowning, I asked, "Where else would I be, Selena?"

"*Right,*" she sighed, almost nervously before rushing me off the phone with a casual, "Catch you later, Dre."

After the call ended, I sat there for a minute, trying to figure out if I was reading into things too much or if Selena was really acting strange. But then I considered what today meant for her and knew it was the kind of moment all ballers dreamed of, cutting her some slack as I found some breakfast, got dressed, and grabbed my bag to leave; making it all the way to the arena only to be bum-rushed by random reporters waiting to ask me questions.

"*How long have you and Selena been dating?*"

"*Is your relationship with Selena the only reason you were hired by the Nymphs?*"

"*Are you using Selena to clean up your Nashville image?*"

"The fuck?" I asked with a scowl, staring down at the puny, blonde reporter who'd been bold enough to even ask me that stupid ass question.

Because of my aggressive response, he'd shriveled a little in his stance before pushing his phone towards my face and asking the question again. And honestly, I wanted to knock his ass out for doing so, making the decision to continue into the arena instead since the last thing I wanted to do was be even more of a distraction as the Nymphs set out to make history in winning the title.

Still, even with good intentions, that didn't mean I had much control of the situation, Katianna being the first to greet me with an extremely hostile, "Why didn't you answer any of my calls?!"

Without breaking stride, I shrugged and answered, "Because I already knew what you were going to say, and I wasn't tryna hear that shit first thing in the morning."

Of course that didn't make her happy, her scowl tight when she growled, "I'm your employer, Dre. You don't get to just blow me off."

"Well as my employer, you also don't get to harass me about my personal life. So where do we go from here?" I asked, stopping to see her face that was twisted up with all sorts of unnecessary anger and annoyance that kept her from responding right away.

Instead of adding more fuel to the flame, I put a hand to her shoulder to say, "Look, Kat. Your franchise is three wins away from making you the youngest owner with a championship-winning team in all of professional sports. Let's just focus on that, aight?"

I could tell she wanted to say more on the subject of Selena and I. But because the rest of the team and staff were slowly beginning to show up, she didn't, giving me an unenthusiastic nod before pulling away to greet them all with a plastered-on smile. And since I was standing there, I did the same, surprised that Mikayla was the only one to mention what was happening on the internet when she said, "Sorry about the poll, Coach. If I would've known it'd become the talk of the finals, I would've never done it."

With a nod, I replied, "I appreciate that, Mik. But it's not your fault. People were gonna talk regardless."

"True," she agreed with a nod of her own. "But just know, if anybody tries either one of y'all, I'm ready to go to war. Y'all are like family to me now, and no one messes with my family."

Considering Mikayla was known for being goofy as hell, it was interesting to see how serious she was about this, yet another thing I could appreciate as I dapped her up and said, "You a real one, Mik."

Receiving the love, she left me with a supportive pat to my shoulder, clearing the way for Selena who'd just squeezed into the door with her hood tied tightly over her head like she was trying to be incognito. And after stopping to have a quick word with Kat about who knows what, she made her way over to me, all smiles as she gave a friendly, "Hey, big baby."

"Hey yourself," I replied, giving her an innocent shoulder hug before asking, "You okay? They didn't do you too bad out there, did they?"

Shrugging, she loosened her hood and pushed it from her head, showing off the pair of *AirPods* she had in when she answered, "I had Jayde playing in my ears. So even if they did, I missed it thanks to the honky tonk bullshit I know you secretly love so much."

"Smart move," I told her, checking out the two new French braids she was rockin' before I complimented, "I'm feelin' this hair though."

There was something sexy and simple yet bad-ass about the look, giving her an extra edge that was softened for the moment when she explained, "Ari came over a little after you called this morning to hook me up."

"Oh, so she gets to interrupt your game day routine, but I can't?"

Chuckling, she made a move towards the locker room and insisted, "I couldn't be out here lookin' raggedy on the big stage, Dre."

"You never look raggedy, Selena."

"You're supposed to say that," she gushed, stopping at the locker room doors to put a hand to my arm and add, "But it's appreciated."

We usually didn't get to have these kinds of moments before games, forced to stay lowkey so we wouldn't tell on ourselves. But now that everything was out in the open, I was taking advantage, grabbing her by the chin when I told her, "Hey. Whatever happens tonight, just know I'm already proud of you. Unless you lose, *then…*"

"Don't play with me, Dre," she giggled before snatching out of my hold with a heavy sigh. "Honestly, though. I've never felt like this before. Never felt like I was playing for something so much bigger than me."

Even though I knew she'd competed in high stakes games before back in college, doing it on a professional level was new territory, bringing its own set of worries that I did my best to address when I advised, "No need to add any extra pressure to yourself, Selena. Just do what you know best and let the universe handle the rest."

That must've been exactly what she needed to hear, her facial expression transforming from one of uncertainty to one of determination right before eyes as she gave a nod before heading into the locker room to get dressed. And from there it was all business, Selena locked in as she ran through her usual pregame routine with that same energy and let it carry into the game that was something like her personal highlight reel.

I mean, the girl was everywhere. Making tough shots on offense, going after every rebound, diving on the floor for loose balls. She was playing scrappy without being out of control. She was talking shit and backing it up. And most importantly, she was being a leader on the floor, directing people to their right positions, giving little tips during every timeout, checking her teammates whenever they started to complain but also the first to give praise whenever something good happened.

As coaches, we couldn't have asked for anything more from her. But somehow, she still found more to give, doing any and everything necessary for the Nymphs to win game one. And as I stood off to the side watching her prepare to do her postgame courtside interview with Bleu Taylor, I was literally beaming with pride until Selena randomly rushed off the makeshift set with her hand over her mouth.

Like I would know what was going on, Bleu shot me a look of confusion that I met with a similar look before taking off after Selena down the tunnel, catching up to see her just as she bent the corner into the training room. And by the time I actually made it into the room, she was already leaning over a trash can with Ari rubbing her back, getting rid of what looked like break-fast and lunch along with the *Gatorade* she'd sipped on throughout the game.

Now I was really worried.

Had all that extra work she'd put in tonight caught up to her?

Was she coming down with something?

Did this have anything to do with how tired she was during the semi-finals?

So many questions ran through my mind. But with Selena still dry-heaving, I knew I wouldn't be able to get an answer right away, instead stepping in to takeover for Ari who quietly said, "I'm gonna leave you two to talk."

Her calmness was eerie, almost like she already knew more than I did about what was going on with my girl. And that only made my anxiety skyrocket as I rubbed Selena's back and demanded, "Baby, tell me what's goin' on."

She didn't respond with words, only stood up and moved to a nearby sink to rinse her mouth with water. And by the time she was finished, she already had tears in her eyes, the unfamiliar sight making my heart pound as I watched her gnaw on her lip before she pushed out, "Dre, I'm… *we're…* pregnant."

"*What?*"

Through her cries, she rushed out, "I know. It's crazy. And what shitty timing, *but…*"

"You're pregnant?" I asked, still in shock as she moved my way with a slow nod.

"I'm pregnant, Dre. Six weeks. Or I guess more like seven now…" she replied, averting her eyes like she really had to think about it.

Either way, I still had plenty more questions, starting with, "How long have you known?"

"Not long at all," she answered. "I found out right around the same time you were traveling between here and St. Louis. Ari set me up with a doctor, *and…*"

"So she knew before I did?" I asked, her immediate

nod in response making sense of Ari's calm demeanor from earlier.

"I didn't want you to freak out. I didn't want... *any of this*. I just wanted to play these games and deal with it later. But clearly the baby disagrees with that plan since, *well*, here we are."

For the first time in a while, it felt like time was standing still as I tried to process everything she was saying - that she was pregnant, *with my child*, now two wins away from one of her ultimate life goals. She'd carried that big ass secret into today, *and balled her ass off*, even through the drama of our relationship going public. And she'd planned on keeping it that way until after the finals; not to be malicious, but to protect *me* from freaking out as if it was even possible for her not to have gone through the ringer of emotions on her own when she first found out.

Honestly, the shit had me blown away on so many levels. But apparently, I was too into my head about it all since Selena moved to stand directly in front of me and urged, "Dre, say something."

Scrubbing a hand down my face, I struggled to find the words. "I'm just... *wow*. A baby. We're having a baby. I mean, if that's what you want of course."

It would've been a little selfish of me to assume her plans since it was her body, her career, her... *everything* on the line. But I also would've been lying if I didn't admit how relieved I was to watch her nod and reply, "Yes. It's what I want, Dre."

My shoulders sank, but only a little since our circumstances were a bit more complicated than that. Even if it came first on the priority list, I wasn't in Selena's life as just her boyfriend. And because of that fact, I had to ask, "But how are you gonna keep playing?"

Like I'd asked a stupid question, she frowned. "What do you mean? The same way I did tonight."

Thinking back on just how hard she'd gone, along with the way her body had reacted to it after the fact, I felt even more protective than normal when I questioned, "That can't be safe, can it?"

With an enthusiastic nod, she gushed, "*Completely*. The doctor I went to already cleared me to do so as long as we continue to monitor everything."

"Nah, we need a second opinion," I urged, Selena somehow finding room to chuckle and sniffle all at once even though I was dead serious.

I wasn't taking any chances no matter how many facts Selena dropped after asking, "Will you relax? Women compete pregnant all the time; run marathons, play volleyball, swim. Hell, when Serena won the Australian Open, she was even further along than I am."

"Everything you just said doesn't involve contact, Selena. And we're not talking about some shootaround in the backyard with friends. We're talking about the WNBA finals. The intensity is on a whole 'nother level."

We were only one game in, but I wasn't sure if I could take watching Selena put herself through all this for another two to four depending on how the series went. But I quickly realized it wasn't up to me when she ranted, "Nothing is keeping me from this moment, Dre. I don't care if I have to puke between quarters, receive oxygen at halftime, and get an IV drip after games. I've worked too damn hard to stop now. *I'm…* I'm too close to the finish line."

Saying it out loud made her burst into more tears, falling into my arms for a hug that I wrapped her in tightly as I told her, "*Shhh*... it's okay, lil' baby. I got you. I'm not going anywhere."

Because of the way her face was buried against my chest, her sobs quieted a little, her voice muffled when she cried, "This just wasn't in my plans. And I'm sure it wasn't in yours either, *but*..."

"Doesn't matter," I interrupted. "It's happenin', and we're gonna be just fine. You, me, and our baby will be fine. I got us."

Whether she believed me or not, she accepted it for now, relishing in my embrace as I kissed the top of her head and repeated, "I got us." And that was enough to bring her quiet sobs to more of a murmur, leaving me with a lot to consider as far as my future with the Nymphs went.

NINETEEN

GAME TWO LEFT me questioning everything.

We'd gotten blown out on our home court, tying the series at one with the odds in our opponent's favor since the next two games would be on their home floor in Seattle. And honestly, just the thought of traveling out there had me exhausted, wondering if it was really all that worth it to keep pushing myself to the limit like this; wondering if it was the best decision for my and the baby's health even if the doctor claimed I couldn't cause any real harm.

On a medical level, maybe not. But mentally, I *just…* wasn't as convinced, sitting with that uncertainty the entire trip to Seattle. And even when we were on the court the next day, ready to fight and take back the lead in the series, I couldn't shake it, making a bunch of uncharacteristic mistakes during the first quarter that had Sugar on my neck trying to talk some sense into me.

If only she knew.

By halftime, we were down by double digits and I took most of the blame by default since I was the one who was supposed to be leading the charge, controlling the tempo, bringing the intensity and getting everyone on my level. But tonight, I just didn't have it in me. And because I didn't have it, we quickly found ourselves down two to one in the series against a now very confident Seattle team.

I was sick.

Everything I'd worked so hard for was in arms reach and I was coming up short. I was giving as much as I had, and it still wasn't nearly enough. I was... *failing* on so many levels by not capitalizing on the physical sacrifice I was making to compete. And with every game, I could tell Dre was becoming a little less confident in my decision to continue playing, making me second guess myself with a do-or-die game four on the horizon.

Was it worth it?

The question played over and over again in my head as I sat in my hotel room weighing the pros and cons, a knock on the door the only thing stopping me from making an actual handwritten list. But when I took a look through the peephole, I was a little surprised to see who was on the other side, skeptical as I pulled it open and asked, "What's up, Coach?"

"Let's talk, Sharpie," Sugar replied, inviting herself in before I could do it myself. And because she was on the shortlist of people - *read: her, Dre, and Ari* - who could do so and get away with it, I closed the door behind us and followed her over to the couch she'd already made herself comfortable on, not all that surprised when she got straight to the point of her visit.

"Tell me what's going on with you."

Shrugging, I lied, "I don't know. I guess I've just lost my mojo."

"Don't bullshit me, Selena. I've seen games where you haven't played your best basketball, and this isn't that. This is something different."

She was right.

This *was* something different.

Unchartered territory that had me releasing a heavy sigh before I gave her a generic explanation. "I'm just really in my head about a lot of things right now, Sugar. But don't worry. I promise I'll be ready for game four."

To me, it sounded like a solid enough response. But Sugar read right through it, putting a hand to my knee to suggest, "You know you can talk to me about anything, right?"

On a surface level, there were plenty of things I'd feel comfortable talking to Sugar about. But unfortunately, this wasn't one of them, forcing me to put on a brave face as I nodded to reply, "I appreciate that, Coach. But I'm fine, really."

Once again, I expected that to be good enough for her to leave it alone. And once again, I was wrong as hell, Sugar popping up from her seat to snap, "Selena, you don't have to be so damn tough all the time. I mean, it's obvious you're trying to hold everything in, carry the world on your shoulders, look like you have it all together. But I can tell you don't. We can *all* tell you don't."

Frowning, I asked, "Who's we?"

"That's not the point," she groaned, squatting down in front of me to say, "The point is that, whatever you're bottling up is showing out there on the court whether you like it or not. So you might as well just free yourself and let it out."

I don't know if it was her words, or her intense gaze,

or a combination of both. But either way, the truth came out like vomit when I blurted, "I'm pregnant."

"Oh shit," Sugar hissed, moving back to her seat next to mine where she asked, "How pregnant are we talking here, Selena?"

"Around seven-ish weeks now."

"And the father is…?" she trailed, leaving a blank for me to fill-in like it was even a question.

In fact, I found myself a little annoyed about it when I replied, "I think you know the answer to that, Sugar."

As if that part was still news to her, she gave a surprised, *"Wow,"* standing up to pace the room and repeat, *"Wow. Wow. Wow. Wow,"* before finally stopping in front of me to ask, "Okay, well what can I do to support you?"

It wasn't the response I expected, so I was a little caught off-guard by the question, gnawing on my lip before I pushed out, *"Umm…* let's start with not telling anyone. I don't want the pity. I don't wanna be used an excuse. I just wanna ball. I wanna win."

With how heavy it had been on my mind before she showed up, speaking it out loud made me emotional all over again. But I appreciated Sugar doing her best to put me at ease when she agreed, "So let's just do that then. Let's go out, get this next win, and force a game five in Nashville. Then we'll win that one, get the title we both want, and you and Dre and the baby can live happily ever after."

Her plan sounded perfect, but it also didn't seem rooted in reality, a frown on my face as I pouted, "Easier said than done, Sugar. I mean, you've seen how I've played these last two games. I don't know if I have anything left."

It was like I was running on fumes, and not just physically. There was no gas in my emotional tank, nothing left to fuel my mental tank. Everything was exhausted, ready to shut down if I went on any longer. But according to Sugar's response, I was exactly where I was supposed to be, a bit of a grin on her face when she explained, "Pregnant or not, no championship is easy to win. You have to dig deeper than you've ever had to before, invest double the amount of blood, sweat, and tears, leave it all on the court. I mean, it's either that or regret not doing so for the rest of your life, and I know you don't want that."

Just the thought made me mad at myself for even considering throwing in the towel. That wasn't who I was, what I stood for, nor who I was raised to be. And that attitude wasn't what had gotten me here, so why in the hell did I think it would keep me here? How could I let my confidence in my abilities begin to waver and somehow still expect the same level of success?

Before I could respond, there was another knock at the door, Sugar giving me a pat on the shoulder on her way to open it. And once she saw who was on the other side, she couldn't wait to tell him, "Congratulations, papa," Dre looking a little confused as she squeezed past him out of the door.

"So Coach Daniels knows about the baby, huh?" he asked on his way over to the couch, taking Sugar's seat and pulling me under his arm to rest against his chest.

Early on, I'd teased him about how awful he'd be to cuddle with. But these days, I couldn't get enough of it, tucking myself a little tighter into his embrace and letting the scent of his cologne soothe me as I answered, "Yeah, it just kinda came out."

I expected him to feel a way about me sharing the news. But to my surprise, he wasn't all that bothered, only shrugging as he kissed the top of my head and replied, "Well she kept the secret about us smashin'. I'm assuming this won't be any different."

"We can only hope," I sighed, less concerned with the possibility of her spilling the baby beans and more concerned with what I was going to do differently next game as I gave more thought to the message she'd left me with.

It wasn't necessarily what I wanted to hear. But it was exactly what I needed to hear, giving me a major energy boost that I couldn't wait to take into game four. Though it was clear Dre was still stuck on the result of game three when he asked, "You feelin' okay?"

"I wasn't. But I feel a little better now," I told him, sitting up to explain, "Sugar put some things into perspective for me."

Nodding, he agreed. "Yeah, she's good for that."

"Better than good," I thought, turning his way to share, "I have to leave it all out there, Dre. I mean, this could be my only chance to win a championship, and I *just*… I don't wanna have any regrets.

"Selena, you are way too fuckin' talented for this to be your only chance at winning a championship," he insisted with a bit of a chuckle that made me roll my eyes as I muttered, *"Says the guy who won one and never even made it back to the playoffs."*

I wasn't trying to be mean, but the facts were the facts. No matter how easy certain dynasties made it look, returning to the finals year after year was no easy feat; let alone returning to the finals and actually winning it all. There were so many things that had to go right, so many injuries that had to be avoided, and in my opinion, the shit required a bit of luck too. But because of the complicated circumstances surrounding his *non-*return, it was easy for Dre to defend, "My situation was a lot different than this though."

"True, but still. We don't know what this baby is gonna do to my body, if and when I'll be back on the court, or if I'll even be the same player. I mean, of course it would be ideal for me to have the baby and be whipped right back into top-tier player shape for next season. But the reality is, that might not happen. I may never make it back to this stage. This could be my last shot."

By the time I finished my spiel, there was a lump sitting in the back of my throat, the emotions of it all coursing through me as I considered every part of what I was getting ready to take on.

Game four

Pregnancy and giving birth.

A comeback.

Motherhood.

Game four.

It was so much to think about, so heavy of a load. But when Dre gently cupped my cheek and chin, it was as if he was letting me know I had someone I could lean on every step of the way, a determined look in his eyes when he finally replied, "So let's make it count."

The phrase, *"Now or never,"* had never meant as much to me as it did in this moment, the National Anthem practically turning into static as I let Sugar's pregame notes play back in my head even though tonight wasn't really about strategy.

No, tonight was all about instincts, about drive, about *heart*.

If I played with heart, the rest would come.

If I played like I was truly driven to do whatever it took to win, others would too.

Everything I'd ever learned about the game was for this moment, so now wasn't the time to overthink.

Now was the time to just do.

From tip-off, that was my attitude, going after everything I wanted instead of letting the game come to me. And because of that approach, we found ourselves within striking distance by halftime, only down five points after Seattle went on a bit of a run to end the second quarter.

Honestly, I was just gassed; though I refused to come out of the game no matter how much Sugar and Dre insisted I did since there was no way in hell I was leaving even a second of this up to chance. And thanks to the extended rest at halftime, I was able to regroup, fighting for every bucket until we were tied up going into the fourth.

Up until this point, being on their home court hadn't felt like some crazy disadvantage. But now that we were in the final quarter and things were still extremely competitive, it seemed as if their crowd had turned up the volume a few notches, doing all sorts of chants that I did my best to drown out and play through. But unfortunately, because of the extra noise, it became a lot harder for us to communicate with each other on the floor. And with that came errors, causing me to miss Mikayla calling out a screen at half court that felt equivalent to crashing straight into a wall when I was blindsided by one of Seattle's players from behind.

I heard the referee blow her whistle to call an offensive foul, but it sounded so far away. I heard the murmurs of boos from the crowd in response, but none of it sounded crisp or clear. And I could hear my teammates celebrating my efforts, but it felt like I couldn't get up to join them, huffing out shallow breaths as Mikayla stood over me and asked, "Selena, you good?"

The nod I gave in response must not have been convincing enough since Mikayla was quick to wave over the trainers. And it wasn't long before Ari was kneeled at my side asking me where I was hurt and advising me to breathe.

In my head, I *was* breathing. In fact, the only thing I could hear were my short exhales and my fast-thumping heartbeat, choosing to focus on that when Ari asked the question again.

"Where are you hurt, Selena?"

Nothing in particular on my body was in real pain, so I didn't know how to respond, only shaking my head as I worked to catch my breath. And after a couple of long blinks, Dre appeared, kneeling down next to Ari with the most worried look on his face until she told him, "I'm pretty sure that screen knocked the wind out of her. She'll be okay. Just give her a minute."

Yes.

A minute.

"Just one minute and I'll be good," I thought, taking only a few seconds before I attempted to sit up. And once I was upright, there was a chorus of sympathy claps from the crowd as Ari and Dre helped me up from the ground

then guided me over to the bench - *the last place I wanted to be.*

There were four minutes left in the game and the only way I could ensure we'd get the win was by being out on the court to make it happen. But no matter how much water I drank, no matter how many breathing techniques I used, and no matter how hard I tried to will myself to *just…* be okay, my body refused to cooperate, forcing me to sit and watch as my team went into the final moments of war without me.

Honestly, not being able to contribute hurt just as bad as a real injury would've; though I tried my best to stay positive as my teammates fought to gain a one-point lead going into the final twenty seconds. And now it was really now or never, Seattle calling a timeout that would advance the ball to half court and give them an opportunity to win the game on a last second shot.

Instead of running through scenarios for what to do based on whatever play Seattle was drawing up, Sugar completely disregarded her clipboard in favor of shouting, "I want you in their faces! Leave them no room! If you need to switch, call it out! If you see a screen coming, call it out! Its loud as hell in here, but we can be louder! This game is ours to win!"

Everyone nodded to agree, *including me*, even though I knew I couldn't do anything with the fire her speech had stoked inside of me. And I was only reminded of that fact when the buzzer sounded and I watched my teammates make their way back onto the court while I stayed on the sidelines, my nerves frazzled as Seattle set up their play before inbounding the ball.

The clock was ticking in slow motion, though something on the court changed with every second. A player moved, the ball was passed, a screen was set to create some space. But again, because of the noise, there was a miscommunication on our end, leaving one of Seattle's players with a wide open three-pointer that had me covering my eyes with my jersey since there was no way in hell I could actually watch that shit go in.

Except... it didn't go in.

The disappointed groan from the crowd told me that. And when I pulled my jersey from my eyes, it was just in time to see Talia securing the rebound, my limbs flooded with relief when the final buzzer sounded meaning we'd pulled it out.

We'd *actually* pulled it out.

The series was now tied, and we were headed back to Nashville with only one win standing between us and the championship. And even though it was the same win Seattle was chasing - *even more so now that they'd blown their chance tonight* - I was feeling a little more confident about it, determined to get back in good health so that I could lead us to the ultimate victory.

TWENTY

ACCORDING TO THE INJURY REPORT, Selena was listed as a game-time decision. But I knew there was nothing - *absolutely nothing* - that was going to keep her from playing in tomorrow's game.

Not the scare in game four.

Not the baby growing inside of her.

Not the "second opinion" doctor who'd suggested she play limited minutes.

Not *me*.

And somehow, that only made me love her even more; a perfect example of her fierce personality that had me intrigued from day one.

Of course back then, she was using all that fire and passion to talk shit about my hiring; to talk shit about me in general. But since that first interaction, we'd grown to respect each other, we'd established a friend-ship, we'd fallen in love. So this time around, I knew it was nothing personal.

She just wanted to win.

And I wanted that for her.

In fact, that was the only reason I was respecting her request to sleep alone, knowing it was an important part of her process to stay distraction-free. But when my phone buzzed in the middle of the night with a text from her that contradicted the usual, I became especially concerned, frowning as I sat up in bed to read it again.

"Can you come over? I need you." - SeSa

Considering the circumstances and how late it was, I knew whatever was going on must've been serious. So instead of wasting time texting back and forth about the details, I hopped out of bed and typed out the only thing that mattered.

"On my way." - Dre

Since I stayed closer to downtown and Selena stayed out in the suburbs, it was almost a half-hour later when I showed up. But regardless of how long I took, she was still happy to see me, falling into my arms the second I stepped inside her crib and asked, "What's the matter, lil' baby?"

Because her face was buried against my chest, her words came out a little muffled. But what I was pretty sure I heard was, "I don't know if I can do it, Dre."

"Do what?" I asked, a bunch of different things

running through my head until she pulled her face away to clarify.

"Play in tomorrow's game. I don't think I can do it."

My eyes went wide at that before drifting into more of a squint, knowing something must've *really* been going on for her to have come to this conclusion. And while my first thought went to her health and the baby's, I tried not to make any assumptions, cupping her face to ask, "Why not? What's wrong?"

She wouldn't look me in the eyes and that only made my concern skyrocket, watching as she gnawed at her lip before she finally glanced back my way to quietly admit, "I'm too afraid."

Her vulnerability struck me deep, knowing it had never been all that easy for her to be open. But the fact that she'd come to me about it spoke volumes. And now that the door to her thoughts was already cracked, I decided to step right in and ask, "Too afraid of what?"

"Of failing, *losing*, hurting myself or the baby, having an irremovable stain on my legacy," she listed. "There's just so much riding on this one moment in time. I don't know if I can handle the pressure."

It was an honest place to be in, letting a tiny drip of uncertainty turn into a full-blown flood the longer you let it run through your head. But even with that, I knew she was still at an advantage, moving my hands to her waist so that I could wrap her in a hug and remind her, "Selena, you've been working towards this one moment for your entire life. And I know it feels like everything is stacked against you right now, *but...* this is when you really get to show what you're made of. Not when everything is coming easy and going right, but when shit gets so hard to the point of feeling borderline impossible."

"I'd much rather it be easy and going right," she muttered with a subtle roll of her eyes, making me chuckle as I agreed, "We all would, lil' baby. But that's not the reality. The reality is, the shit we want more than anything is usually the shit we have to work the hardest for. And sometimes, that work is more mental than physical cause the physical part is already in you. Baby or no baby, you know how to ball."

I wasn't sure if it was the mention of the baby or the mention of her being a baller. But either way, my words made her crack a smirk when she nodded to reply, "You're right. I'm trippin'. It's your child's fault. Has me all in my feelings."

Again, I chuckled. "Nah, leave my baby outta this. This is between mom and dad," I told her, the title "dad" making my chest warm as I thought about everything it represented.

It was the greatest responsibility; giving me new purpose, yet another reason for me to continue to fight old habits, something else to live for and look forward to. And as I looked down at the woman who was making that possible, I felt overwhelmed with gratitude; though she was the one to actually express it when she said, "Thank you for always showing up for me, Dre. It means more than you'll ever know."

"Wouldn't have it any other way, SeSa," I replied with a kiss to her forehead. "Now let me get outta here so you can get some sleep. I know how you are about your routine."

I was already making a move for the door when she caught me by the arm to say, *"Actually,* I'd love it if you stayed. I could use some of those infamous cuddles."

Naturally, my eyebrow piqued at her request. "Do

you think that's a good idea? I mean, I don't want you blaming me for throwing you off if, *for whatever reason*, shit goes wrong tomorrow."

The possibility only made her shrug, taking full responsibility when she pulled me closer and replied, "Nah, tomorrow will be all on me. Tonight, I just want you."

With that, there was nothing more to be said, Selena leading the way towards her bedroom where she climbed into bed then waited for me to get rid of my clothes so I could join her. And once I did, I quickly learned she wasn't lying about her desire for my cuddles, hardly settled into the perfect resting spot spooned against me before I heard the soft murmurs of her snoring.

In this moment though, there was no sound in the world I'd rather here, nowhere in the world I'd rather be. So with a kiss to the back of her head, I whispered, "Love you, lil' baby" before dozing off to sleep.

The moment had come.

Winner-take-all game five.

A chance to make history.

And my last game coaching for the Nymphs.

I hadn't shared the details of that with Selena just yet since there was already enough on her plate and she needed to stay focused. But with the news of the baby, taking the Trojans job was a no-brainer; especially since Selena would be missing the overseas season and then only be receiving a partial salary from the WNBA until she returned.

Honestly, I didn't want her to have to rush. Even with her potential endorsement money, I wanted her to be good regardless; wanted us to be comfortable regardless. And with the extra money I'd make with the jump from the WNBA to the NBA, I could guarantee both of those things; though a jump to the Trojans also meant dealing with the likes of Kage Steele who'd just shown up to the game rocking my girl's jersey.

Crazy enough, I wasn't even mad at him. Selena was unbiasedly the best, and if I was just a normal fan of the team, I'd probably be wearing her shit too. So instead of reading into his choice of attire too deeply, I gave him a, *"What's up"* nod on my way to the locker room and kept it pushing, glad when he did the same thing back without any extra fanfare.

The simple interaction had me thinking the upcoming season might not be so bad after all. But for now, that was going in the back of my mind since tonight was all about the Nymphs, all about Selena, all about finishing the job and getting that title. And when I saw my girl sitting in her locker spot with her game face on, I knew shit was about to get real as we both listened to Sugar's pregame speech, got hyped with Mikayla, then stayed back for our little handshake and kiss ritual before Selena took off to follow the team.

At least, that's what I thought she was doing until she stopped at the door, turning back my way to say, "Oh, and Dre?"

Lifting my eyebrows as if to ask, *"What?"* I was surprised when she responded with a grin, completely out of the ordinary for moments like this. But it made sense in combination with the words that caught me even more off-guard, my chest tight when she gushed, "I love you too."

When I said it last night, I assumed she was asleep and didn't hear me. But now that I knew she had and that she felt the same way, today felt even more special, a smile on my lips as I told her, "Go get what's yours."

That seemed to lock her right back in, one single nod being the only thing she responded with before leaving to join the team. And because this was my last go-round, I took my time following her, savoring every moment on my way out to the court that was rocking with noise thanks to the packed-out crowd decked in cardinal red and silver.

I wasn't sure what kind of fandemonium the Trojans were bringing in these days, but I knew it was nothing like this, the enthusiasm reminding me more of a college atmosphere than a professional. And this time with it being our home crowd instead of Seattle's, the squad was able to use the excitement as fuel, giving us a comfortable ten-point lead that allowed Selena to get a little rest on the bench going into the second quarter.

Unfortunately, with her out of the game, that lead dwindled from ten to two in no time. But once Selena got back in, everything changed, lil' baby taking that message of showing them what she was made of to heart with every bucket she scored on offense, every steal she got on defense, and all the little things she did in between to give us the advantage going into halftime.

"Two more quarters, ladies. Two more quarters and that title is ours," was the base of Sugar's message; a simple yet effective approach according to the fire we came into the second half with. But Seattle came with a little fire of their own, causing us to trade baskets back and forth until we found ourselves all tied up going into the final quarter of the game.

It was intense, with neither team going away easy. And with so much at stake, that was expected. Everybody was playing their asses off and everybody was tired, but no one was giving up. And of course that included Selena who was all sweat, a little bit of blood thanks to a few random scratches on her arms, and tears I assumed she was holding back since she wouldn't dare shed them on a stage like this.

Not until she finished the job.

With twelve seconds left on the clock and possession of the ball after Seattle threw it out of bounds, we found ourselves with an opportunity to do just that, Sugar calling a timeout to draw up a play that would break the tied score and give us the win. But when she charged "Sharpie" with the task of taking the last shot, I saw Selena visibly panic, shaking her head as she insisted, "It doesn't have to be me. It can be someone else."

"No, Sharpie. I trust you," Sugar pressed, moving on to recap everyone else's job on the play. But my focus was on Selena who still didn't look quite sure of herself, only halfway listening as another assistant coach went on some pseudo-motivational spiel before the buzzer sounded signaling the end of the timeout.

Before she could hit the court, I caught Selena by the arm to remind her, "It's already in you." And even though she nodded to let me know she'd heard me, I still wasn't sure how well she'd actually absorbed my message, my heart pounding as I watched the Nymphs set up exactly what Sugar had drawn up before inbounding the ball.

It looked like Mikayla was wasting time as she dribbled at the top of the key. But really, she was just patiently waiting for everything to play out the way Sugar had written up. And with five seconds left, Selena popped open off a screen from Talia, Mikayla throwing the pass with perfect timing and giving Selena a clean look at the rim for a shot that soared through the air in slow motion before nicking the inside of the hoop and popping back out.

Shit.

Even though it wasn't the end of the world since it only meant we were headed into overtime, I could tell it felt that way to Selena, her head down as she stood in the same spot she'd taken the shot from with her hands on her hips in defeat until Mikayla threw her arm over her shoulder to guide her off the court. But even when she returned to the bench, her jersey was pulled over her mouth as she looked to be fighting back tears, Sugar giving her a bit of tough love when she advised, "Save the waterworks, Sharpie. This game is far from over."

Just like with me, Selena gave Sugar one of those empty nods as Coach went on to explain our approach for the extra period. And with the sound of the buzzer, Selena was forced to either go big or go home, lowkey doing a combination of both as she shared the load of the overtime fight with her teammates who were all playing their best ball leading into yet another tied game going into the final moments.

This time around, Seattle had possession of the ball, giving them an opportunity to burn the shot clock and win the game on a last second shot. But with no time-outs left, they had to play it out without being able to draw up a specific plan, giving us a bit of an advantage on defense as our girls stayed in their faces with Sugar yelling out a reminder, "No fouls! No fouls!"

The clock was ticking down and Seattle had yet to get a clean look at anything, giving me the assumption that they were okay with going into a second overtime. But when one of their players went for a slick backdoor cut towards the rim late in the shot clock, I thought they'd gotten us until Mikayla stepped in to intercept the pass, securing the ball and throwing it up court to Selena who must've predicted the steal considering how open she already was.

I mean, there was literally no one within a few steps of her as she dribbled on a fastbreak towards our hoop. And with the clock running out, she went up for an easy lay-up that bounced into the rim just as the buzzer sounded, the arena going up as the bench cleared out to storm the court in celebration.

As coaches, we stayed back to hug each other as the team created a dog pile on top of Selena in the middle of the floor. But the second she could make it out, she did, dashing over to me to jump into my arms and plant the biggest kiss on my lips like she didn't give a fuck who was watching.

I for sure didn't give a fuck, savoring the salty taste of her lips as she pecked me over and over again before whispering against them, "We did it, Dre."

"*You* did it, Selena. This was all you. So fuckin' proud of you."

My face was wet with a combination of her tears, her sweat, and *shit*, a little bit of my tears too. But I wasn't ashamed to cry happy tears for my woman, understanding what this moment meant to her now and would mean to her forever.

No matter what happened with the rest of her career, with the baby, with *us*, she would always have this to call her own. And that deserved to be celebrated, though I still found room to tease, "I think you might've broken the curse from that shit I did back in high school with that lay-up you just made to win the game. Think you might've redeemed our family."

I was really only messing around since that miss way back when had nothing to do with her. But in this moment, she could do nothing but smile, licking her lips to repeat, "Our family. I like the sound of that."

EPILOGUE

IT WAS CHRISTMAS DAY.

And instead of spending my time playing in some meaningless game overseas or lounging at home alone in comfy pajamas, I was sitting in the family and friends' section at the Trojans game, happily cheering my man on as he did nothing but hold a clipboard.

He looked good as hell holding that clipboard though. The best clipboard holder in the whole NBA, making a ridiculous amount of money to do just that which meant I was going to support him every step of the way.

But really, it was about a lot more than just him holding the clipboard. It was about him doing what was necessary to provide for our growing family. It was about him finally being welcomed back into the league even if it wasn't as the player he once was; a comeback that a lot of people didn't see for him considering the way he'd left the game. And it was about him making the most of his opportunity with the Nymphs that had turned into this opportunity with the Trojans; one of my favorite things to tease him about since that meant I'd successfully kicked him out of our league.

Bottomline, I was proud of him. And I was proud of us. And I was happy to be showing off my cute little baby bump that we'd just gone public about with a cheesy holiday-themed post on *Instagram;* a post that had been picked up by *ESPN*, Spilling That Hot Tea, and every page in between.

Surprisingly, the response had been all positive, the media speaking on it for the love story that it was instead of the scandalous shit it could've gotten filed under. But even if they had gone that route, I was too enamored to care, still riding the high of the championship to let any internet troll kill my joy.

The championship.

Somehow, it still didn't feel real; like that game five had been a dream instead of the very hard-fought victory that it was. But honestly, I wouldn't have had it any other way, happy to have shared such a special moment with the two people I loved most; Jordan DeAndre Leonard and our big head baby who seemed to be growing by the hour.

With that growth came an appetite out of this world, so I was thrilled when I saw Jayde finally returning from the concession stand with another source of joy - *food*. A while back, we'd made plans to have wine and catch up. But since I obviously couldn't do that anymore and Jayde had her own reasons to be at the game, this worked out perfectly, Jayde handing a tray my way as she said, "Alright, Champ. Here's the nachos you said you wanted; jalapenos on the side cause I wasn't sure if baby Leonard liked it spicy or not."

With a giggle, I thanked her as we both settled in for

the second half, a smile on my face as I watched her watch her favorite player do his thing. And because I knew how happy they were together, I couldn't help rubbing my stomach and teasing, "You know y'all got next, right?"

"*Girl.* Do you see how big that man is? I already hurt from hole to hole just thinking about it," she joked, the both of us cracking up laughing as we tuned in to the rest of the game.

Thankfully, the Trojans pulled off an easy win, keeping the holiday spirit flourishing as Jayde and I made our way down to the court to catch up with our men. But before Dre could even get to me, Kage stepped up to tease, "You know that baby should've been mine, right?" making me chuckle as Dre teasingly pushed him out of the way from behind.

After the drama between them during the Nymphs season, it was cool to see how they'd grown to take a liking to each other, Dre apparently seeing something in Kage that reminded him of himself coming up. But to me, they were *totally* different, making me grateful for my decision early on to not pursue one in favor of letting things play out with the other who was currently wrapping me in a hug to ask, "How you feelin', lil' baby? You good?"

"I'm excellent."

"You look excellent," Dre complimented with a smirk, planting a kiss on my lips before telling me to stay put while he ran to the locker room. And now that the crowd had mostly cleared out, it somehow felt eerie being on the court like I hadn't just spent an entire season here; I suppose because my body knew it might be a while before I got back.

Maybe if we hadn't won the title this year, I'd be more pressed about my return. But because we had, I was honestly looking forward to my break away from the game. I mean, basketball had been my world for so long, the only thing I really cared about, the only thing that ever received my undivided attention. But now I had some new things to give that same energy to, a smile on my face just thinking about it until I saw my baby daddy jogging out of the tunnel changed out of his designer coaching suit into a replica of my Nymphs uniform.

"Dre, what the hell?" I giggled, watching as he grabbed a ball from the rack to dribble my way.

"You owe me a rematch. Check up," he answered with a hard bounce pass in my direction, the ball landing perfectly in my hands before I propped it against my hip to respond.

"Dre, I am not about to play you."

"Why not? You scared?" he challenged, clearly trying to get under my skin.

But I wasn't falling for it, only smirking as I told him, "Don't test me."

Of course, instead of accepting my request, he did the exact opposite, shaking his head while he taunted, "Get one little championship and now you runnin' from the competition. *Damn*. You hate to see it."

"Dre…"

"Nah, it's cool," he insisted. "If I were you, I wouldn't wanna play me either."

"Ah, fuck it," I groaned, dropping the ball to my feet to remove the jacket I had on while asking, "What are we playing to?"

"Same as last time," he answered excitedly before

reminding me of our rules. "First to five, counting by ones and twos. Make it, take it."

"Bet," I agreed, finally checking the ball up to start our game. And for us to have been just messing around, I still broke a little bit of a sweat, quickly realizing that I was a lot further along than I had been the last time I picked up a ball as I scored point four of five.

"Game point, big baby. You better guard me," I taunted, catching the ball he'd passed to me on a check-up before I turned around to back him down to the rim. But when I put a little umph in it on my pursuit of the hoop, Dre flopped, falling to the ground with claims of an offensive foul that had me turning around to argue the call until I discovered he was on one knee.

The ball became irrelevant since I needed a hand to cover my mouth, bouncing off to nowhere as Dre grabbed my free one to say, "Selena, I am and will forever be your biggest fan. You've been a bright spot in my life, a perfectly-timed gift from God, a challenge in the best way possible. And I love you for it. I am *in* love with you. I'm in love with what we're becoming, and if you'll have me, I wanna make it official."

I was touched on so many levels, but somehow still found room to joke, "If?"

"You kinda hardheaded, *so…*" he teased, catching a smack to the shoulder that had him cracking up laughing before he pulled a ring box from his pocket and continued, "Nah, in all seriousness. Selena "SeSa" Samuels, will you marry me?"

Like he truly didn't know what I was going to say once he opened the box, there was this adorable nervous glimmer in his eyes as he gave me some time to think it over. But really, there was nothing for me to think about.

We were already bonded, already a team. And there was no one I wanted on my squad for life more than Dre, grinning my ass off as I answered, "Absolutely."

With a grin of his own, he slipped the ring on my finger before hugging himself against my belly. And while the moment brought tears to my eyes, the fact that we were in the middle of playing for game point before this all happened reminded me, "*But wait.* We still have to finish our game."

There was no way in hell I was letting him escape taking a loss like he did the last time, not even after his beautiful, thoughtful, pussy-wetting proposal. But when he stood up from the ground just to look down at me and lick his lips, I realized it no longer mattered, feeling so in love when he replied, "Nah. I already won."

THE END.

EXTRAS

Enjoyed this book?
Please leave a review on Amazon or Goodreads!

To stay up-to-date with all of Alexandra Warren's happenings including samples and excerpts, visit actuallyitsalexandra.com, like her Facebook page, or sign-up for her newsletter!

Also, be sure to check out the *One Last Shot* playlist on Spotify and Apple Music!

ALSO BY ALEXANDRA WARREN

Attractions & Distractions Series
Getting The Edge
An Unconventional Love
The PreGame Ritual
Distracted
The Real Deal
A Rehearsal For Love
An Encore For Love
Love at First Spite
In Spite of it All
Accidental Arrangements
Heated Harmonies
If Only for the Summer
In His Corner
The Games We Play (FWB Book 1)
The Lessons We Learn (FWB Book 2)
Wins & Losses
Building 402 Series (Book 1-3)
A Tale of Two Cities Holiday Collection
Baggage Claimed

Made in the USA
Middletown, DE
14 June 2020

97783114R10155